Sam Felt As If All The Breath Had Been Knocked Out Of Him.

He counted back and realized it was a full three months since their night together.

Lila was going to have a baby. That would explain her contradictory actions, one minute flirting and the next throwing an invisible wall between them and refusing to go out with him.

Had she come to Texas and expected to avoid telling him? Anger stirred that she would hide the truth. Maybe she was going to wait until she was back in California to let him know.

She had to realize she couldn't hide it forever.

A baby. Their baby. He *would* marry her.

Deep in a Texan's Heart

SARA ORWIG

First published in Great Britain 2013
by Mills & Boon, an imprint of Harlequin (UK) Limited.
Large Print edition 2013
Harlequin (UK) Limited,
Eton House, 18-24 Paradise Road,
Richmond, Surrey TW9 1SR

© Harlequin Books S.A. 2013

Special thanks and acknowledgment to Sara Orwig for her contribution to *Texas Cattleman's Club: The Missing Mogul* miniseries.

ISBN: 978 0 263 23797 9

SARA ORWIG

lives in Oklahoma. She has a patient husband who will take her on research trips anywhere, from big cities to old forts. She is an avid collector of Western history books. With a master's degree in English, Sara has written historical romance, mainstream fiction and contemporary romance. Books are beloved treasures that take Sara to magical worlds, and she loves both reading and writing them.

Thanks to Charles Griemsman,
Stacy Boyd and Allison Carroll.

Thank you to a special group
of writers: Maureen Child,
Kathie DeNosky, Tessa Radley,
Yvonne Lindsay, Jules Bennett,
Janice Maynard, Sarah Anderson
and Charlene Sands.

Thanks to readers for their support,
enthusiasm and friendship.

One

When Sam Gordon idly glanced over the crowd at the annual Hacket barbecue, a head of straight auburn hair caught his attention. It could be only one person. Lila Hacket's silky hair was a unique color, a deep auburn shot through with red strands as natural as the rest of Lila. She was back in town and his pulse jumped over the prospect. Had she come home for the barbecue? Memories of Lila heated Sam's insides while the horse conversation faded, replaced by memories of holding Lila's warm, naked body against his.

The ranchers around him laughed over something Beau Hacket said, so Sam smiled, trying to pick up again on the conversation. Beau proudly pointed out his latest acquisition, a three-year-old sorrel, to the Texas Cattleman's Club members gathered beside the corral.

Standing with her back to him, Lila chatted with another group of guests. She was taller than several women around her. She wore a turquoise sundress that had narrow straps and a top that came down over her hips, hiding her tiny waist. Her feet were in high-heeled sandals and she looked luscious. Certain he would talk to her before the evening was over, Sam attempted once more to focus on those around him. Local cattle rancher Dave Firestone and gray-haired energy magnate Paul Windsor quizzed Josh, Sam's twin, on horses. Josh loved horses, one more thing Sam didn't share with his twin.

"Beau, did you get that horse around here?" Chance McDaniel asked.

"No. I drove to a sale in Cody, Wyoming. But that isn't the kind of horse you need on your dude ranch."

"My place is a working ranch, too, and I'd like

to have another cutting horse," Chance replied, his green-eyed gaze roaming over the horses.

"Chance, you need some horses like the little mare I have for Cade. Something gentle even a four-year-old can ride," Gil Addison, another local rancher, added.

Sam was not involved with horses but most of the men in his circle were horsemen one way or another, from Ryan Grant, now retired from the rodeo circuit, to rancher Dave Firestone. All belonged to Royal's elite Texas Cattleman's Club and Sam saw them often enough that he didn't mind breaking away from the group.

"Y'all excuse me," Sam said. "I'll be back." He strolled away in an easy stride that belied the anticipation bubbling in him. When Lila had not returned his call the morning after their one-nighter, he had let it go. There were other women in his life. That had been three months ago—three months in which he couldn't shake her out of his thoughts.

Why was she back in town? Laughing, she moved away from the people standing around her.

Determined not to lose her, Sam walked a little faster through the crowd.

It took only another minute to catch up. "Lila, welcome back."

When she turned, there was an almost imperceptible flicker in the depth of her crystal-green eyes. "Sam," she said. In spite of her smile, there was no warmth in her voice. "I hope you're enjoying the party," she said, sounding as if they were polite strangers and had never shared a night together. This was not a reaction he usually had with women.

"This is a great party, as usual. Better now that you're here. Did you come home for the barbecue?"

"No, as a matter of fact. I'm in town to set up for a movie that'll be filming on ranches here at the end of the month," she said. "It's nice to see you again. Enjoy yourself at the party." She turned slightly to greet her longtime friend Shannon Fentress, still thinking of her as Shannon Morrison, instead of Mrs. Rory Fentress since her recent marriage.

"Hi, Shannon. Just welcoming Lila back to town," he said.

"It's the first of August, just in time for her family's big annual party—who would miss this? I think all of Royal is here," Shannon said. "Lila, that barbecue is the most tempting smell ever. Too bad they can't bottle and sell it like perfume."

Lila laughed. "C'mon. We have a new chef. You can meet him. 'Course, my dad is going to supervise. Excuse us, Sam," she said sweetly, motioning to Shannon to follow her.

Sam watched them walk away, his gaze raking over Lila's back. Her cool reception had been a first for him. He didn't get that reaction from women. He frowned as he watched the slight flare of her hips, the sexy swing to her walk. As he studied her, he wanted to go out with her.

He shook his head and turned to go get a cold beer. Lila didn't take after her dad. She didn't even seem much like her mother, who was friendly, always happy to stay in her husband's shadow, to be the wife in the background. In her own quiet way, Barbara Hacket kept Beau happy, entertained constantly and had charity projects without ever showing the streak of independence Lila did—that need to get away from Royal, to have a fancy job. Lila and her brother, Hack, were light-years apart.

As if his thinking about Hack had conjured him, Sam greeted her brother as he approached. "Great party, as always, Hack."

"Dad knows how to have a barbecue. Saw you talking to my snooty sister," Hack said.

"Snooty is okay. At least your sister's kind of snooty is. It may not run deep," Sam replied, still watching Lila as she disappeared into the house with Shannon.

"Like a challenge, huh?" Hack said, rocking on his heels and hooking his thumbs over his hand-tooled belt. "Guess you're right. Chicks are easy. Sometimes it's sweeter when there's a challenge because most chicks are so eager they're boring."

Lost in thought about Lila, Sam barely heard Hack.

"My hotshot sister is home from L.A., where she thinks she's setting the world on fire with her highfalutin movie job," Hack continued. "She's living alone out there—or so she says—probably because no one will live with Miss Snooty. It gives me more money from the old man. My sister can just stay in California. It's a good place for her. Royal, on the other hand, does have the hot chicks. Think so, Sam?"

"There are fine people in Royal, Texas," Sam said, his thoughts still only partially on Hack.

"Speakin' of hot chicks, I see Anna June Wilson. If you'll excuse me," Hack said, walking away.

Sam took a deep breath, glad Hack had moved on. At seventeen, the kid was spoiled rotten by Beau. Sam had seen Hack around his dad. The kid was smart enough to keep on Beau's good side most of the time. The rest of the time, Beau bailed him out of trouble.

Sam raked his fingers through his hair and strode to the outdoor bar on the large patio. After Lila had returned to California, he'd called her. When she hadn't taken his calls, he had stopped phoning. Was she cool because he hadn't continued to pursue her? He should forget Lila Hacket. Trouble was, he hadn't been able to forget Lila.

"Dammit," he said under his breath.

"Sam Gordon, what are you doing standing by yourself?"

"Just looking for you, darlin'," he said, smiling at Sally Dee Caine, the perfect antidote for Lila. Known by every male in Maverick County, Sally Dee was fun and Sam enjoyed her in small doses. He took in her bright pink, low-cut, clinging jersey blouse and tight faded jeans. "You look good enough, Sally Dee, to make me forget about the enticing barbecue that's cooking. I might find what I want right here," he said, nuzzling her neck. Giggling, she wrapped her arm in his.

"Sam, you're usually a partying fool. C'mon, the fiddler's wound up and there's a barn filled with two-steppers dancing the time away."

"I thought you'd never ask," he said, grinning as he draped his arm across her shoulders and pulled her close against his side. While she slipped her arm around his waist, they headed toward the Hackets' big brown barn.

"Sorry if I interrupted you if you wanted to stay and talk to Sam," Shannon said as she walked beside Lila.

"No, you rescued me. I know you don't care to meet the barbecue cook. Let's head for the dining room. We can get some of Agnes's artichoke dip."

"Your parents' cook is the best in Maverick County."

"She's good, but we have a lot of good cooks around here. Also, I saw her carrying a tray of gorgeous fruit into the dining room."

"Yum. I won't argue that one. It's great to have you home. As usual, your family's barbecue is fabulous. Each year, this barbecue seems to be bigger than the year before."

"I think it is bigger. Nearly all the Texas Cattleman's Club members are here. There's an undercurrent this year, though. I hear people talking about Alex Santiago's disappearance. That mystery has some on edge."

"No one knows what happened to him and they're keeping publicity about it to a minimum, I think. Or maybe they just really don't know anything. It's odd and it's scary. No one, much less a member of the Texas Cattleman's Club, just disappears."

"Alex Santiago did."

Shannon shivered. "I hope they find him soon. I understand that he's a wealthy investor—who knows what he's involved in? What about you? You said you're on vacation for two weeks?"

"Yes. I have to be here in two weeks anyway because the studio will be shooting a picture in the area. I took two weeks off beforehand. I'm working a little, trying to select locations, but I'm taking some private time for myself."

"Your work sounds like a dream job."

"Sometimes it is. It can get hectic, but I'm learning and I like what I do."

"You have two weeks' vacation." Shannon's blue eyes focused on Lila. "Why don't you think about squeezing a little time to help plan the new child center at the Texas Cattleman's Club? We could use your professional opinion. The construction company is renovating the place, but they want the women's input about the decor and what we'd like to have for the children."

Lila laughed. "My dad would explode. You can't imagine—well, yes, you can imagine—how he feels about a child center. It almost did him in when women were voted into the club, Shannon," Lila said with a big grin.

Shannon laughed. "I love being a member of the club. I still can't get used to women, including me, belonging to the exclusive male bastion, the sacrosanct male domain for over one hundred years, the exclusive Texas Cattleman's Club." She laughed again with Lila. "I better not speak loudly—all the members are here tonight.

"I know it irritates your dad and some of the others," Shannon continued. "Your dad and a lot of the older members, but some young ones, too. The Gordon twins. Your brother has made snippy remarks."

"I told you years ago to tune Hack out. Dad spoils him until it's pitiful. I'm afraid Hack is going to turn out as narrow-minded as Dad. If you weren't such a good friend, I think Hack would make worse remarks to you. He can get really crude."

Shannon shrugged. "I do tune out your brother and the remarks are more than just snippy. He isn't going to like the child center. Doesn't matter. The construction company has already started renovation."

"That's great."

"Lila, you're perfect for the job because you're a production set designer. C'mon. Help us while you have some time."

Thinking over the request, Lila looked into Shannon's bright blue eyes beneath short, sassy blond hair. Lila had come home to rest, to talk confidentially with her mother, not to take on another job. If she accepted, though, it might keep her mind off her problems and it would be an interesting project. She would be with Shannon, a hard worker who was always fun. "You know, I'd enjoy collaborating with you and the idea is exciting. Besides, sometimes I like to shake up my dad. I'll do it, but if it gets to be too much, Shannon, I'm out."

"Fantastic and fair enough. I don't want you to participate if it's too much, but it won't be. I'd like your input."

"That sounds easy."

"It should be fun to do. Any chance you can meet me at the club Monday morning?"

"Sure. My schedule is open. As long as it's not early Monday morning."

"No, we won't meet early, because I have my ranch chores," Shannon said as they walked down a wide hall into the big dining room that had a table holding silver trays and crystal dishes of hors d'oeuvres.

"Hi, Amanda, Nathan," Lila said while Shannon echoed her greeting to the couple, who stood holding hands and had been gazing at each other until they were interrupted. Amanda and Nathan Battle, Royal's sheriff, turned to look at them. Lila felt an invisible punch in her middle when she saw them holding hands, clearly in love.

"The newlyweds," Lila said, smiling at them. "Congratulations."

"Thank you," they said in unison, then looked at each other and laughed.

"We were just taking a moment away from the crowd to talk. The party is fantastic, Lila. Your folks know how to throw a party," Amanda said. Amanda's glow and obvious joy continued to give Lila a pang. What would it be like to be deeply in love, to have it returned? From the way Amanda looked, it seemed it would be bliss.

"We'll head out to get some barbecue," Nathan said.

"Don't go on our account," Lila told him. "We're here for some artichoke dip and then we're going outside to eat."

"Eat all you want," Nathan said, smiling and wrapping his arm around Amanda's waist as they left.

"They're so much in love I doubt if either one of them knows what was just said or even who was in here. Now, I think we were talking about getting together at the TCC Monday," Lila said.

"We were. Actually, the later the better for me. How about lunch? While we eat, I can bring you up to speed on what we plan. After lunch we can go look at the location. It's the old billiard room."

"That will be good. Lunch will be the best time for me," Lila said, crossing to the sideboard to pick up a plate and napkin.

"At three on Monday, there is a TCC meeting and I plan to attend, but you and I will be finished by then," Shannon said.

"I'll bet my dad is suffering over the thought of turning the billiard room into a child-care center." Lila laughed and Shannon joined her.

"It's time to shake them up a little," Shannon said. "Besides, they'll get a new billiard room. That renovation will be next."

"Shannon, do the Gordons have the construction contract?" Lila asked, realizing for the first time that she might see a lot of Sam.

"As a matter of fact, no, they don't."

"Why not? I'd think they would have been awarded the contract without any conversation about it," Lila said.

"I wondered about that, too. I was told they bowed out because of a 'conflict of interest,' but frankly, in my opinion, they wanted to avoid it because they hate to see the center become a reality."

"Could be. The Gordon brothers are as old-fashioned as my dad."

"Maybe they're that way because they lost their mother when they were so young. Perhaps their dad just settled into a chauvinistic manner toward women."

"Probably. Even with a mom, my dad's influence, unfortunately, is stronger on Hack than my mom's."

Lila and Shannon browsed, each selecting small bites of the pale, steaming artichoke dip and dainty bits of pineapple, strawberries and kiwi. As soon as both had tall glasses of ice water, Lila waved toward the wide hallway. "Let's go sit on the porch, where we can talk. Everyone's in the back or in the house."

They walked outside on the porch and sat in tall cushioned rocking chairs. The music was diminished, the sounds of the crowd muffled, while shadows grew longer and the sun slanted lower. "You look great, Shannon. Married life becomes you."

"You have to meet Rory. Right now he's back in Austin. My foreman is ill and I'm needed here, so I'm at the ranch."

"You're newlyweds, very happily married. What else? Bring me up to date on your life," Lila said.

Shannon shrugged. "While I'm here, it's just the same old, same old. I run the family ranch," she replied, raking her blond hair from her face with her fingers.

"I don't know how you do it," Lila said, shaking her head. "I've never figured out how you manage the Bar None all on your own."

"Just one of the boys," Shannon replied dryly, and Lila laughed. "I'm not alone anymore, not since getting married. It's just that Rory is busy in Austin."

"Too bad you have to be apart."

Shannon shrugged. "When my foreman is back on his feet, I can go to Austin. Right now, this is a rare moment, this party, and I'm enjoying it. I've told you about me. Let's talk about you, unless you don't want to. We're good friends or I wouldn't ask—what's wrong?"

"Wrong?" Lila said while her heart missed a beat.

Shannon shrugged. "If you don't want to talk about it, I understand. I thought you might need a friend right now."

Shocked that Shannon could so easily tell that something was wrong in her life, Lila ran her fingers in a circle over her knee and debated confiding in her friend. So far her mother was the only Texan she had talked to.

"All right. It's confidential for now. Since I'll be here anyway in a couple of weeks, I came home early to rest and talk to Mom. Not my dad. Never Hack. I'm pregnant, Shannon."

"Great grief." Shannon's eyes widened. "Someone in the movie business? An actor? A star? A producer who's married?"

"Hey, wait," Lila said, laughing and feeling a lift to the worries that weighed on her only moments earlier. "Stop jumping to conclusions. A married producer? I wouldn't go out with one of those. I shouldn't have gone out with the man I did," she said, becoming somber again. "Shannon, he's local. He's here at the party."

"You don't have to say who it is. Are you going to tell him?"

"Not until I make some decisions. When he finds out, he's so old-fashioned he'll want to marry me."

"Oh, great grief. If it had to be a local, why didn't you pick someone who's open and liberal and not still thinking a woman's place is in the kitchen and bedroom?"

"Hindsight is always better."

"I'm sorry. I'm not helping. I can understand why you don't want to marry him, but if he's old-fashioned, he's going to want to marry you. Oh, boy, is he going to want to marry."

"I'm not marrying one of the locals to move back here and give up my career and my independence."

Shannon tilted her head to study her friend. "When are you breaking the news?"

"I wish it could be after I'm back in California and there's half the U.S. between us, but I'll probably tell him before I go back. Okay—absolutely between the two of us. It's—"

"Don't tell me," Shannon said, covering her ears. "I don't want to know."

Lila laughed. "You do make me feel better. I can tell you and you'll probably guess anyway."

"No. I don't need to know. I don't even want to know, because it will be easier later if someone gets to quizzing me. You know, you can keep that quiet only so long," she said, glancing over Lila. "I guess that's why you're wearing a dress that covers your middle."

"That's right. I'm three months along."

"Oh, my. How long will you stay in Texas on this movie-production business?"

"Probably till the end of the month. Sometimes it's shorter, sometimes longer, but once I start really working, I don't think I'll see the significant person often."

"Does your mom understand? Your dad isn't going to."

"She's supportive. I don't even understand what got into me."

"I think it's called hormones," Shannon remarked dryly. "And he's probably adorable because we have some good-looking, fun, great guys here."

"Oh, yes," Lila replied, thinking that was a fitting description of Sam. "As for Mom, we're close. Mom has two sides to her. The one my dad sees and others think she is, and then there's a side that's not that way at all. Mom manages to get her way with my dad. He just doesn't realize it. She'll help me."

"Good. Sorry, Lila. You've complicated your life."

"That's an understatement. Thank heavens I can leave Royal and go back to California."

Two men emerged from the front door and turned toward them. Lila recognized both of them as ranchers from a neighboring county.

"Hey, ladies," Jeff Wainwright said. "I thought I saw you two out here. You're missing the fun and a really good hoedown in the barn. Right now they're having line dancing. Want to give it a whirl?"

Impulsively, Lila accepted, thinking it would be good to move around, expend some energy and forget her pregnancy for five or ten minutes.

If only she could forget. The first sight of Sam had taken her breath. She had thought she wouldn't have any physical response to him, but she had been wrong. Worse, she had been unable to control her response. With a sparkle in his clear blue eyes, he'd stood facing her. His navy plaid Western shirt had the sleeves rolled high, revealing firm biceps. The shirt tucked into his narrow waist and the faded tight jeans showed his muscled lean frame. He looked sexy and filled with vitality—a good-looking, appealing man. She couldn't deny that part.

Also, it had felt good to tell Shannon about the pregnancy, to have a friend who knew what she was going through. And a level-headed friend, too.

In minutes Shannon was dancing with Buck McDougal while Lila danced with Jeff. Sam was on the dance floor with Piper Kindred, one of Royal's paramedics. As she turned, Lila noticed the ex-rodeo rider, Ryan Grant, on the sidelines watching Piper intently. Lila looked away, thinking about how she tried to avoid watching Sam or even looking at him, but it was impossible. He was light on his feet, sexy. It didn't matter how much appeal he had—his personality, his opinions, his most basic beliefs all were opposite from her own. He was old-fashioned and would never understand her career or her attitude.

She thought about that night with him. Her dad had seen Sam in Royal and talked him into dinner with them in town. When Sam had said he would take her home, her dad had gone ahead to the Double H, her family's ranch. She and Sam had flirted through dinner and afterward, until Sam invited her to his place for a nightcap and she accepted.

The flirting grew more intense until she was in his arms. A night of wild passion, laughter, loving, a night she had known she would always remember. Now there was no doubt. A few weeks later, she had learned she was pregnant.

Lila's thoughts came back to the present while she danced in the barn. They had gone from line dancing to a square dance and she noticed Shannon had dropped out and was gone.

They square danced, changing partners as the steps were called out to the fiddlers' music. When they called "Promenade left, promenade right," and she moved to the next dancer, she faced Sam and the look in his eyes made her heart pound. He wasn't saying a word, yet sparks flew and she felt at any second he might grab her and kiss her wildly.

She danced away from him and the moment was gone, but her heart still raced and she wondered if they would talk again or if he would ask her to dance. She gave a shake of her head as if to clear her thoughts. She needed to stay away from Sam. She didn't want him to guess that she was pregnant. She had to be mentally prepared for when he learned the truth.

Finally, she told Jeff she'd had enough dancing. As they left the barn, she glanced back and met Sam's smoldering gaze. Even with the length of the barn between them, the minute she looked into his eyes, a current spiraled, tickling her insides. Why did she have such a physical response to him? She did not want to know Sam better or go out with him again. Yet now she had not only bound her life with his indefinitely, she would have to struggle with his old-fashioned, narrow view of the world.

The tempting smells of the barbecue were beginning to have the opposite effect on her. To get away from the cooking, she crossed the yard until she saw a friend.

"Sophie," she called, catching up with her high school friend.

Sophie Beldon turned to wait, her light brown eyes friendly as she smiled. "This is a great party, Lila. Your family really knows how to do this. I think everyone in these parts looks forward to August because of your family barbecue. It's legendary."

"Thanks. They've been doing it long enough. It's good to see you. Where are you headed?"

"Some quiet corner—if there is such. I'm getting looks and people ask all sorts of questions. Some act like I have the answers and just won't say anything about Alex's disappearance."

"Sorry. That must be tough. You're his executive secretary, so everyone probably thinks you know something about him. I'm sure everyone has been shocked to hear Alex has disappeared. Still no word?"

"Nothing. What's bad—they don't know whether something's happened to him or his disappearance is something he has deliberately done. He had a quiet side where he kept things to himself. I've always thought of my boss as a man of mystery. Or it could be just circumstances where communication has failed and Alex thinks we all know where he is."

"That seems impossible. You'd hear from him, I'd think."

The blonde shrugged. "Who knows. You can't rule out any possibility, but his disappearance has some people on edge."

"Reasonably so, I'd say. You dealt with him daily. You should know the most about him," Lila said, stopping in the shade of a tall oak to the east side of the house and away from the crowd.

Long lashes framed Sophie's eyes while her brow furrowed. "I get looks from Nathan Battle, but Nathan's fair, so I'm not worried about his opinion where I'm concerned. I really don't have any idea about Alex and what's happened to him." She studied Shannon in silence a moment as if debating something. "I know I can trust you— I'm working now for Zach Lassiter. He's Alex's business partner."

"I've heard Dad talk about him. From what I hear, no one seems to know much about his past."

"Talk about a man of mystery—Zach is more mysterious than Alex was. I don't think anyone knows much about Zach. I thought if I could get close to him, I might find out something about Alex's disappearance."

A chill ran down Lila's spine. "Sophie, be careful. You have no idea what's involved in Alex's disappearance. It could be foul play. You really don't know anything about Zach Lassiter and it sounds as if no one else in Royal does. What you're doing might be dangerous."

"I'll be careful, and I don't see how Zach can suspect my true motives. It's a business. I can't keep from wondering what he knows about Alex, because they worked closely together."

Lila shook her head. "I don't think you should take such a risk. Be really careful about what you do. You're not a trained detective and you don't know anything about investigations. Does anyone else know what you're doing? Does Nathan Battle?"

"Heavens, no. You do now, so there's one person who knows. I promise, I'll be careful. I see friends headed our way."

Lila turned to see three more friends she had been close to in high school and her private conversation with Sophie ended, but as she listened to the light chatter of her friends, she still had a nagging concern about Sophie. She wished she had urged Sophie to say something to Nathan, although Nathan and Amanda had recently married, so he might not have his mind on Alex's disappearance. Still, Lila felt certain Nathan would advise Sophie to stay out of it and her friend might actually listen to him.

Later, lines formed at the long tables covered with food while servers at each end carved chunks of meat and ribs. Lila went inside to eat more fruit, passing up the steaming barbecue, knowing her dad saw to it that they cooked so much there would always be some leftovers if she wanted any later.

After dinner, fiddlers swung into music for more dancing and Lila enjoyed herself, dancing with many of the Texas Cattleman's Club members who always attended the Hacket barbecue. She danced with Ryan Grant, one of the newest members. His tangled brown hair fell over his forehead as he concentrated on dancing. He was light on his feet, which didn't surprise her, because she had danced with him before.

The next dance was with rancher and widower Gil Addison. She knew his four-year-old son,

Cade, was with the other kids. Her parents always hired local nannies to watch the small kids
during the barbecue. She enjoyed Gil in his quiet
way and was sorry he was raising his son alone.

As soon as that dance ended, Sam's twin, Josh
Gordon, politely asked her to dance. She could
sense the coolness and disapproval in spite of his
invitation and she knew he was one of the club
members who disapproved of her independence.
She suspected he had asked her to dance as an
obligation to her dad, the host.

Although Josh and Sam were identical twins,
Lila could tell them apart without any difficulty.
Sam's hair was longer and he had a sparkle in his
eyes, a more carefree attitude than his solemn
brother.

As she danced with Josh, a fast number where
they had no physical contact, she wondered what
his reaction would be when he learned that he was
going to be an uncle.

As soon as the dance ended and she had politely
thanked him, Josh disappeared into the crowd.
She turned to face Sam Gordon.

Two

"I think it's my turn. Will you dance with me?" he asked, taking her arm before she could answer.

"This is typical, Sam. You didn't even wait for my answer."

He grinned and released her, turning to face her. "Darlin', you can't begin to guess how eager I am to dance with you. Miss Hacket, may I have this dance?"

Knowing Sam was the one person she should avoid, she nodded her head anyway. "You're hopeless."

"No way, sugar. I just want to dance with you in the worst way," he said, taking her hand and coaxing her. "C'mon."

"In the worst way?" she teased, having fun even though she shouldn't encourage him.

"Oh, yeah," he drawled in a huskier voice as they joined the dancers on the barn's makeshift dance floor. "The very worst—down and hot as only you can do," he said.

A tingle sizzled while she laughed at the same time. "Not on your Nelly, Sam Gordon," she tried to reply sternly, but it came out breathlessly. "I don't even know how."

"Oh, yes, you do, darlin'," he said, his blue eyes twinkling. "My memory is crystal-clear. In the privacy of my place, we've danced down and dirty before and it was a bushel of fun and sexy as hell." He moved closer. "And you haven't forgotten, either."

"If you want to keep dancing, Sam, you better get off that subject fast. You've skated onto extremely thin ice," she said, wishing she sounded more forceful and knowing she had made a big mistake in flirting with him even for mere minutes, not to mention dancing with him.

He waved his hands as if he had dropped a burning iron. "I'm off the subject of how enticing your dancing is. You look great, Lila, and I'm glad you're home."

"Thank you," she said, twisting and turning so they wouldn't have to talk, yet aware of his steady gaze following her every move. She should never have encouraged him, but he was fun to be with and she loved to dance. Thinking like that was what had gotten her into the situation she was in now.

The instant the music stopped, she turned to him. "Thanks, Sam. Mom asked me to mix with guests. I've just mingled with you, so I'm off to socialize with others," she said sweetly, and walked away before he had a chance to reply. Her back tingled because she knew he watched her and she expected him to catch up with her or take her arm to stop her.

As if pulled by a magnet, she couldn't keep from glancing over her shoulder. Sam was leaning against a post on the sidelines and he was watching her as she had suspected. She turned around quickly, but he had seen her look back at him.

As she moved through the crowd and toward the house, she fought the urge to glance over her shoulder again. Her mother had given her no such instructions, but she had partied all she wanted to for one night. She was going to her own room in the sprawling ranch house.

Standing near the bar, Sam watched Lila cross the back porch and enter the Hacket home. As puzzled as ever, he couldn't figure her. For minutes tonight, she had let down that guard and been open, friendly, more—she had flirted with him. And he thought she'd had fun dancing with him. Then it was over and the barrier was back between them. The moment the dance ended, she was gone. Why her coolness? Was it his attitude toward her job and women in the club? That seemed absurd and hadn't made that much difference their night together. He couldn't think of a thing that would cause this rift between them.

She didn't approve of his views of women and he didn't approve of her career, so he should accept the rejection and move on. Rejection was something he didn't experience often—was it that difficult for him to accept? He still wanted Lila in his arms and in his bed.

She had looked great tonight—a flush in her face that made her cheeks rosy, a sparkle in her fascinating green eyes, her long legs showing from the knees down.

The dress hid her tiny waist—a pity because he remembered exactly how narrow it was. But the top of the sundress was cut low enough to reveal lush curves that seemed even fuller than he remembered.

He inhaled and took a long drink of his cold beer, wishing he could just pour it over his head to cool down.

Monday, Lila walked into the rambling clubhouse made of stone and dark wood. Sunshine splashed over the tall slate roof. The smell of bacon cooking wafted from the building, giving her a queasy feeling. Morning sickness had come early and had been mild. To her relief, it was beginning to disappear, and so far, today was one of the good days.

Shannon was waiting in the wide hallway. Dressed in a sleeveless navy cotton dress and heels, she didn't look as if she had spent the morning doing ranch chores with the men who worked for her, but Lila knew Shannon and what her life had been like until recently, single-handedly managing a big cattle ranch.

Shannon's smile sparkled. "Hi! I've looked forward to this since the night of the barbecue. I'm so excited over this child center." She leaned closer to Lila. "I'll warn you now—you're going to get some nasty glares from the members who do not welcome what we're doing."

"I'm getting looks at home from Dad. He grumbles and stomps off without really saying anything."

Shannon laughed as they headed toward the dining room for lunch.

Over crisp green salads, she enjoyed talking to Shannon, listening to plans about the center. "Remember they built onto the club and we have more meeting rooms now, so they moved the billiard tables to one of the meeting rooms. They'll renovate the room later, but for now they just moved out the other furniture," Shannon said.

"It wouldn't do for all those men to be without their billiard tables," Lila said with a smile.

"Right. Meanwhile, they've started on the billiard room and the room built adjoining it. They're taking out the walls that separated the rooms. We'll divide off areas for play, for eating, that sort of thing, and a special area for the babies."

"I know some great California stores for furniture, pictures, little dividers that still keep an open look and can be easily moved."

"Great. Give us a list. The women members are responsible for this. As soon as we eat, we'll go look at the rooms. I told you that we've agreed on the basic structure, which includes built-in shelves, drawers and cabinets. I'll show you all of our plans and notes."

"I'm sorry the other women couldn't join us for lunch. I would really be in good company with you, Missy Reynolds, Vanessa Woodrow and Abigail Price."

"You should join, too."

Lila shook her head. "I'm going back to California. You need members who will be active."

"Abigail's little girl, Julia, will attend the center as soon as it opens."

"It's exciting to be part of this," Lila said, enjoying seeing her friend and having something else to think about in place of the constant concerns about her pregnancy.

When they finished lunch, they went first to the door of the old billiard room. Men were sawing and hammering, and the noise made talking difficult.

Shannon just motioned for Lila to follow her and they went down the hall.

"We can go to the billiard room."

They entered the darkened room with four billiard tables, heavy brown leather furniture and coffee-colored walls. There were two small stained-glass windows. Shannon switched on an overhead light fixture made of deer antlers.

"Looks dark and sort of like pictures I've seen of hotel lobbies in the early 1900s," Lila said.

"They'll redo it, although I think there will still be dark leather furniture and I'm guessing the stained-glass windows will remain. That's not our deal and frankly, I don't care what they do with this room." They sat at a game table in the corner of the room and Shannon spread the papers in front of Lila.

"Here's a list of some child centers that have been recommended to us as the best examples. You can study them and see what ideas you come up with. We want a state-of-the-art child-care center."

"Will the center open onto a play area outside? I don't see a door anywhere."

"Great grief. No one has said a word about a playground," Shannon said, her eyes opening wide. "We may have been so busy campaigning to get a child-care center that we didn't stop to think about outside, but we definitely should have a playground. I'll send Missy a text about this. That's a necessity." She pulled out her phone, speaking into it, dictating her text.

"I don't know why we didn't think of that. We have plenty of space outside and we can have a fenced area with alarms, making it secure for the kids. We'll always have attendants to watch and cameras. We've ordered a state-of-the-art alarm system for an enormous price, but it'll be worth it and give families peace of mind."

"This center is going to be wonderful, Shannon."

"It is, but there's a faction who really opposed it

and they still don't like it. Sometimes that makes me uneasy."

"These are honorable men. For all my dad's bluster, he does have a good heart. He's just old-fashioned but, in his own way, courteous to women and good to Mom."

"I'm sure you're right. I guess this thing with Alex disappearing is disconcerting. Something isn't right and you can't keep from wondering if anyone is in danger."

"Hopefully, they'll learn the truth soon or he'll return. As far as I know, there's been no demand for a ransom."

Shannon shivered. "One of Royal's citizens kidnapped—that's ghastly." She glanced at her watch. "How about meeting here again at twelve-thirty or one on Wednesday? If you can have lunch, great. If not, that's fine, too."

"Actually, one will be better."

"Good deal." Shannon's gaze ran over Lila. "Are you feeling all right?"

"Yes. Mornings are rocky, but then I'm okay the rest of the day. This center is exciting, Shannon. Maybe I'm interested because I'm thinking about children now."

"I'm excited and there's no little one on my horizon. I think it's great. It's almost time for my meeting. Wednesday, it is. Lunch again."

"Fine. I'm going to stay a few minutes here to think about this. You go ahead to your meeting."

"I'm going to see Abigail Price there. She's so excited about this center."

"Very good. Abigail was brave—the first woman to join the club. She'll be in their history whether this bunch of members likes it or not."

"Enough liked it to get her voted in," Shannon said, laughing. "See you Wednesday."

She disappeared out the door. Lila looked at the room, the billiard tables, imagining how many deals had been made over these tables and what a male domain the billiard room had been. It was time for change.

Less than five minutes later Lila walked out and saw a tall man in cowboy boots down the hall. She recognized the broad shoulders and lean frame of Sam Gordon. He stood in a doorway talking to someone and glanced her way. The minute they locked gazes, a reaction shook her. Another jump in her heartbeat accompanied a thorough aware-ness of him. She raised her chin as if meeting an adversary.

As she drew close, he finished talking, stepping fully into the hall and turning to wait for her to catch up with him.

"I haven't seen you here in a long time. Having lunch with your dad?"

"No, I'm not. I met with Shannon today. She asked for suggestions on planning the interior of the child-care center." Lila caught the slight frown that was gone from Sam's expression almost as fast as it had come.

"I can't imagine a child-care center in this club. What I can imagine is the reaction the founders would have had to such a thing."

"Sam, come into this century. The founders were a long time ago. You're way too young to be a fossil."

"I don't remember you accusing me of being a fossil when we danced or kissed," he said, lean-ing closer, "but then, there are some places, Lila, where our different opinions don't matter one whit."

"I walked into that one," she said. "The child center is going to happen, so you might as well get resigned. You don't like kids, Sam?" she asked, feeling a clash of wills with him.

"'Course I like kids, but here in the club—that's a different. This club wasn't founded to babysit a bunch of kids."

"Who was it founded to babysit?" she asked sweetly.

He leaned closer, placing his hand against the wall over her head and hemming her in. Too aware of his proximity and her pounding heartbeat, she drew in a deep breath. "It was founded as a male haven where men could relax and enjoy a drink or a cigar or the friendship of cronies without kids yelling and running through the halls."

She laughed. "Mercy me. You're beginning to sound just like my dad. If I heard you and didn't know you and couldn't see you, I'd guess you were part of his generation."

"That's not all bad, Lila. You go out with me tonight and we'll see if I'm an old-fashioned fossil," he drawled softly, his blue eyes holding fires that sparked.

Lila tingled. She had gotten on dangerous ground with him again. "Thank you, but, Sam Gordon, you and I are generations apart in our lifestyles and ways of thinking, the places where it really counts. Lust is universal. Compatibility is not. I'll see you around," she said, hurrying away, trying to ignore her racing pulse and the stab of longing to go out with him.

He was totally off-limits and she shouldn't have even stopped to talk to him, much less spent time flirting with him. They had little in common, so how could he hold such an intense appeal to her? Worse, now he was the father of her baby. For years to come she had tied her life to Sam's, unless he had no interest when he discovered the truth. She knew just how her daddy and some of the old-fashioned men who were his friends would have reacted to the situation, and that was exactly the way she expected Sam to react. He would want to marry her.

She shivered. She was not marrying, settling for a life like her mother's and living in Royal for the rest of her life. Being the "little woman" in the kitchen and his toy in the bedroom and being

seen and not heard otherwise. No way was she
going to become part of that scene.

She encountered Shannon in the hall. "I thought
you'd be gone now," Shannon said.

"I ran into Sam and talked a minute."

"He's here for the meeting. I've never missed
one since I joined the club, which irritates some of
the good ol' boys," Shannon said, smiling broadly.
"I'm sorry, your dad is one of them. If looks could
kill, I'd be gone."

"That's dreadful, Shannon. I don't even know
why you want to be a member and have to put up
with that."

"There are a lot of benefits. This is the most
exclusive, elegant club in this area, so it's great
for private parties. I can swim, eat here, bring
Rory here—you know they have the best chef and
cooks for miles around. I love the dances."

Lila laughed. "Shannon, when you're here, you
don't have spare time to do anything except ranch
chores."

"When Rory can come and my foreman is well,
I have more time. Rory does a lot. Maybe I can't
resist shaking up the old boys a little," she added
with a grin.

"Go to your meeting and shake them up. I'm going home to the Double H," Lila said, walking away before she ran into Sam again.

Sam relaxed in the meeting room at the Texas Cattleman's Club. He tried to focus on what was being said by Gil Addison, their president, but his thoughts kept slipping back to discovering that Lila intended to help plan the child-care center. The whole idea was repugnant to him. He looked around at the dark, rich wood, the mounted animal heads, trophies of past members and evidence of their shooting skills. The clubhouse was over one hundred years old, now, a monument to being built right and using the best materials.

The club had been a male haven. Leadership, Justice, Peace—the basic founding motto of the members. In an earlier day the club's members had banded together covertly on secret missions to save innocent lives. That wouldn't happen now with all the changes. The club was relaxing, filled with the things he liked to do—swim, dine, play billiards, exercise, just talk with friends. It was the perfect place for business lunches or dinners. Now women had moved into it and changes were coming, but the biggest alteration was a child center. Children racing through the clubhouse and scampering over the grounds would change the ambiance and the noise level would rise like a balloon in the wind. A child-care center. Beau Hacket had been bitterly opposed and Sam, as well as his twin, had lined up with Beau. There was not one positive reason to take children into the Texas Cattleman's Club, but they had been voted down.

Sam glanced across the room at the female members, clustered together, their husbands, mostly younger members. Why did they want to be part of the club? A streak of stubbornness? To ruin the club for the men? To take it over and turn it into their own club? He couldn't figure the logic, but they were not going away. Between their husbands, boyfriends and friends, they had solid backing, not only gaining membership but easily voting in the child-care center. Once they got the center, the club would become a whole different type of organization.

His gaze rested on Shannon. She was Lila's close friend and the one who had talked Lila into helping plan the child center. He liked Shannon; she was a no-nonsense person and a fine rancher. Of all the women who had joined, Shannon probably had the most right to be there because she was a rancher and toiled like the men on her ranch. She ran the place and fit in with other cattle ranchers. A stranger would never guess, because when she left the ranch, she looked all woman.

Lila would help with the center. If she lived here, she would want to join. Beau had definite ideas, but he hadn't been able to control Lila or raise her to live the way her family did. There were probably some stormy conversations at the Hacket house.

Sam tried to stop thinking about Lila except to acknowledge she was taking over too much of his thoughts.

Once again, he tried to pull his attention back to Gil, who stood relaxed, his black hair combed back and one hand holding a small card that he occasionally glanced at.

In his quiet, efficient manner, Gil had covered the business of the day and Sam had barely heard a word.

"I know some of you opposed the new child-care center, but it's been voted in and work has started. During the renovations, we'll have noise and interruptions, but we've had that before. The child-care center is going to be reality in the near future. We want a state-of-the-art center."

Annoyed, Sam thought it would partially be thanks to Lila's input. In fairness, the billiard room would be renovated into a center for kids whether Lila helped or not. The founders of the exclusive men's club would be stunned by this latest turn of events. He thought of Tex Langley, the founding father, who might not have even wanted the club if he had known how it would be changed.

As far as Sam was concerned, the club would never be the same. He attempted again to pay attention to Gil, who seemed to remain impartial, although Gil had Cade to raise by himself, so probably, he was happy to see the center open.

"Another reminder, next month Zach Lassiter will be inducted," Gil said.

Zach was another newcomer and Sam knew nothing about his past except that he had been successful with investments and he had shared an office with Alex Santiago.

Startled, Sam realized he was thinking in the past tense about Alex. What had happened to the man? It was a disturbing mystery that seemed to puzzle everyone in town.

"One last thing before we close our meeting today," Gil said in a loud voice that quieted everyone. "We all know we have a missing member, one of our newest members, Alex Santiago. Nathan has something to share with us," Gil said, turning to face Nathan Battle, who rose.

Tall, with a commanding presence, Nathan made a good sheriff. He was a law-enforcement officer the town could be proud of. The men of his family had been members of the Texas Cattleman's Club for generations and Nathan had broken away from his ranching background to become a lawman. He'd become an asset for Royal.

"This will be brief. We've turned up something. My office hasn't gone public with the news yet and we don't intend to make an official announcement at this time, but I'll tell you now—Alex's truck has been found about fifty miles from town."

There was a low rumble of remarks, with surprised looks on a few members' faces.

As soon as Nathan began to speak again, silence
fell over the room.

"The truck was hidden in bushes. That may indicate foul play. At this point, we're not ruling
anything out. From all indications, there's a possibility that Alex was abducted."

Another shocked ripple of noise erupted.

"Nathan, when will you go public with this? Are
we to keep quiet about it?" Dave Firestone asked.

"We've been investigating and trying to find out
what we can before moving the truck, but several
people already know about our discovery. I'm not
trying to keep our news secret from the town, but
I've asked to keep it out of the media at least the
rest of today. Alex was a friend and one of our
members and I know there's high interest in his
disappearance. At this point, that's all."

Nathan returned to his seat and Gil finished the
business at hand before closing the meeting.

Shocked by the news, Sam thought about Alex
Santiago, a venture capitalist and new to Royal.
He'd grown up elsewhere, without Texas roots

that went back generations the way so many of the other members' did. Newly engaged to Cara Windsor, Alex had just recently disappeared. Word got out slowly at first and then swept over the town. Sam glanced across the room at another member, Chance McDaniel, who used to go out with Cara. Chance sat stony-faced, staring straight ahead, a slight frown on his brow beneath his blond hair.

How bitter was Chance over Cara getting engaged to Alex? Sam had wondered about that since people began to openly question what could have happened to Alex.

Jumping to conclusions wasn't good, but it was impossible to avoid suspecting Chance, who would have a motive for getting Alex out of the way.

At the same time, Sam liked Chance and would hate to see his suspicions bear fruit. He hoped Chance wasn't involved. Finding Alex's truck abandoned and hidden was not good news.

After the meeting when Sam was leaving, he stopped in the doorway of the future billiard room. The place was dim inside with muted sounds from the club, the old billiard tables standing empty. Life was changing. Was he as backward in his thinking as Lila had accused him of being? He shook his head. He couldn't imagine little kids all over the place or that their presence would be great for the club. The TCC could have built a separate building on their property or bought some land near the club and built a separate center and everyone would have been happy. Or at least that's how he and several other members viewed it, but their idea had been killed before it ever got started.

Yesterday he'd had a business lunch and he was glad he could bring a client to the club just the way it was. Time would tell whether the child center was an asset or a liability. Turning to leave, he spotted something on a chair by the door. He walked over to pick up a small stack of papers with a long mailing tube. Shannon's name was on the mailing tube, so she had probably left everything while she attended the meeting.

As he turned to go, Lila entered and stopped. "I left some of my things in here and I came back to get them."

"I just found them. I thought they were Shannon's." He handed Lila the stack of papers and the mailing tube. His hands brushed hers only lightly, yet the touch was electric.

"Did the meeting just get out?" she asked.

"It's been a few minutes. I stopped in to look over the new billiard room."

"I'm sure you'd prefer no changes to this room, just as you prefer no changes to the original billiard room."

"You're wrong there. The room is antiquated and we'll have a new billiard room. I have nothing against little children. You don't know me half as well as you think you do. But now we can begin to remedy that. I'd like to hear all about this California job you have and why California is so much greater than Texas."

"One more big difference between us. I'll be happy to tell you why California is so great— one thing is I can be independent and on my own. That's a little difficult to do here in Royal with my dad constantly present everywhere I go."

"If that's the problem, I can take you someplace where we can enjoy the shade and your dad won't be anywhere around. We can discuss that in the bar or outside on the patio where the mist makers are keeping everyone cool. It's late in the afternoon and it's nice outside if you're in the right place. Come have a drink with me and then I'll take you to dinner. Or even more private, I can take you to my place and I'll guarantee no one will disturb you."

"Except you, Sam. You're disturbing enough," she said, and his insides tightened and heated. Her eyes sparkled and eagerness made him smile.

"Darlin', you take my breath away. You look great, Lila," he said, gazing into thickly lashed green eyes that he could look at endlessly.

"Thank you, Sam."

"C'mon. Let's get that drink. What are we waiting for?"

He could tell the moment the wall came up between them. Her expression changed only slightly, but the sparkle left her eyes and she looked as if she were on the other side of a glass wall. She shook her head.

"That's a tempting offer, Sam, but I need to head home."

As she started to move away, he touched her arm lightly. "I promise. Stay and you'll have more fun. I can take you home later if you want and bring you back tomorrow to get your car."

"Sorry, Sam. Thank you, but I need to get home. I've promised to make suggestions regarding the center for Shannon. I'll see you around," she said briskly. He dropped his hand as she gathered her things and left the room.

Puzzled, he watched her walk away. Why was she avoiding him? There were moments she had been responsive and then she had closed off as if he were a stranger. What was bothering her and what had changed between them since that weekend they had been together? Switching off the lights in the billiard room, he stepped into the hall and slowly followed, still watching her walk away.

They had a big difference in their attitudes about the club and the child center, but he didn't think that was what was holding her back.

At a loss, he watched her go out through the front doors. Was it something he had done? Was it because she was scared to be attracted to someone from Royal and get involved when she lived in California? Not for one second did he think she had to go home to study child-care centers for Shannon. There was something else that had caused the rift.

He couldn't think of a reason. One more puzzle in his life, only this one was personal. While he wanted to get to know her better, she had made it obvious she wasn't going to let him. The only reason he persisted was that she still responded to him some of the time.

Three

Lila hurried to her car. Prickles ran across her back because Sam was behind her and she had the feeling if she turned she would see him watching her. If only she could stop flirting with him. For a moment she had wanted to just toss aside worries and go sit with him and let him cheer her up because he could. In spite of his old-fashioned notions, he entertained her.

She suspected her mother had thought the same thing about her father at some point. Sam was too much like her father for her to get close to him. Yet it was too late. She had gotten up close and intimately personal and someday she would have to let Sam know about his baby, but she wanted to be on the verge of leaving for California when that happened.

Passing mesquite and cactus, she finally curved around the drive and saw the sprawling, familiar house on the Double H ranch. The place would always be home. Pots of colorful flowers hung beneath the rafters of the wraparound porch. Her mother had made a comfortable haven on the West Texas plains.

That night over a steaming roast with potatoes and carrots, her dad talked about his day. Momentarily, Lila wished she had been able to accept Sam's dinner offer, because it would have been far more fun than listening to her dad complain about too many things.

"In our meeting today, Nathan made an announcement. They haven't gone to the media about it yet, so it isn't public knowledge," Beau said, looking at his wife and then at Lila. "He said they found Alex Santiago's abandoned truck hidden in some bushes outside town."

"That can't be good," Barbara remarked, frowning.

"No, it sure as hell isn't," Beau replied. "They're

investigating. Sounds to me like someone kidnapped Alex or worse."

"Was it random or someone who knew Alex?" Barbara shook her head. "I know no one has an answer to that question, but it's disturbing. Your friend Sophie worked for him, didn't she?"

"Works for him," Beau corrected.

"Sophie still keeps the office running. Zachary Lassiter shares the office with them, too," Lila said.

"You be careful, Beau, when you're out on the ranch alone. Until we know who or why—"

"Don't worry about me. My pistol is in the truck and I'm careful. I have my phone and most of the time I'm not out without others with me."

"One of the men disappearing is frightening. Imagine that happening here."

"Things happen everywhere, Mom," Lila said.

"You're the one who lives in a hotbed of crime in a big city," Beau remarked, helping himself to more roast beef while Lila struggled to eat a little. She had lost her appetite, but she didn't want to bring it to her dad's attention.

"We haven't talked about it, but I heard you're

helping with the children's center," Beau said, focusing on her.

"Shannon asked if I would just look over the plans they have and see if I can think of anything else needed."

"A new location would be nice," Beau said, and laughed at his own joke. "It's sort of embarrassing to me to have you a part of this children's center. Actually, sort of embarrassing to the whole family."

"Beau, she's merely looking at pictures and notes to make suggestions," Barbara said sweetly. "Don't be persnickety the little time we have her home with us."

"Yep, it's good to have you here, baby. I wish you'd just get a job in Royal and stay put, marry one of the locals before you meet some Californian and he carries you away from us for good."

"If that happens, I want your room," Hack said.

"Hack, for heaven's sake," Barbara chided. "No. Lila will always have her room and you have a perfectly good room, sitting room and bath that are as large as hers."

Ignoring her brother, Lila smiled at Beau. "It's nice to be home, Dad," she said.

After dinner Beau sauntered away to watch television while their cook, Agnes, cleared the table.

"Mom, I'm going to my room. I'm worn out and I want to look over the material Shannon gave me."

"Sure, Lila. I'll come up in a little while."

In her room Lila switched on her laptop and looked up the best child-care centers in the United States to see what comprised each one. About an hour later she pulled out the plans of what already had been decided on for the TCC center.

Lila began to make notes of a few changes she would make if it were all left to her. A light knock on the door was followed by her mother thrusting her head into the room. "Can I come in?"

"Sure. Want to look at the drawings?"

Barbara crossed the room to sit close to Lila and look at the drawings while Lila pointed out various things.

"Looks very cutting-edge. I'm glad you're helping. How are you feeling?"

"Good. I get tired, but otherwise I'm okay."

"Lila, you're going to have to decide what you'll do. I'd like you to come home to have your baby."

"I don't know, Mom. I'm thinking about it."

"Please come home. I can take care of you and the baby. Also, honey, sooner or later you'll have to tell Sam about the baby. Sam and your father."

"I know I will. I have to tell Sam face-to-face. Hindsight is really great, isn't it?"

Barbara just smiled and waited.

"I have to tell him while I'm here, but I intend to do it right before I leave for California."

"That will suffice. Although I don't think the distance between California and Texas is going to slow Sam Gordon down. Those two boys grew up with a tough rancher father. They built their own successful construction business. Lila, Sam is going to want to marry you. Having raised two children, I want you to think about it before you turn him down."

"Mom, you know what Sam Gordon wants in a wife. A woman like you. You're sweet. You humor Dad. I know you get what you want and Dad doesn't even realize that he's been manipulated—"

"I wouldn't go so far as to say that I manipulate your father."

"Of course you do," Lila said sweetly, smiling. "He can't see it so he doesn't object. But you don't work outside home and he would have a fit if you did. I love my job. I don't want to give it up to come home and live in Royal."

"Just think it over. It's difficult to raise a child, and a single parent has a hard time."

Lila thought of Gil Addison and Cade. Sometimes Gil looked harried, while other times he had a fleeting, forlorn expression—was it the lack of a mother for Cade and a wife for him?

"If you turn him down, you better be ready for a battle. Sam Gordon doesn't strike me as the type to give up. He's eaten a lot of dinners at our house. He's a nice man, Lila."

"I know he is, Mom. That helps."

"And on the subject of announcing your pregnancy—you have to tell your father."

"I told you I will before I leave, but I want to make decisions about what I'll do. Dad will want to take over totally. And there's no doubt he'll want Sam to marry me. I can't bear to think about that one. Also, I don't want to hear Hack's smart remarks."

"I could break the news first to your dad and he will take care of your brother."

"Let me think about what I'll do," Lila said, while she wished she could go right back to California.

Barbara stood and hugged Lila. "Don't worry. I'm glad you're home. Of course, if I have to, I'll go to California when the baby is born."

"I understand."

"Whatever you do, you know I'll back you up."

Lila squeezed her mother's hand. "You're still the best mom in the whole world."

Barbara laughed. "I love you, Lila, and love having you home. I'll go see about your dad now. He was asleep when I came in here."

Lila bent over plans and pictures again. She jotted down ideas as she looked at Shannon's notes. Finally, she shoved them aside to think about Sam. How was she going to tell him?

Wednesday morning, even though she didn't want to see Sam, she couldn't keep from studying how she looked before she left the ranch. She changed twice before finally settling on a plain two-piece dress, a sleeveless green cotton one with a V neckline. Like several newly purchased dresses for the trip to Royal, the top was tailored and came to her hips with a straight skirt below it that once again hid her waist.

She didn't want to run into Sam and have him studying her figure while she was wearing something that showed her waist. She brushed her hair and clipped it up on the back of her head. After a few critical moments in front of her mirror, she was satisfied.

When she reached the club, she spread her plans on the game table in the future billiard room to study them again while waiting for Shannon.

Her cell phone interrupted her and she answered to hear Shannon's voice.

"Lila, I'm sorry. I need to cancel. We have a cow giving birth and having trouble. The vet's on his way. I am so sorry since I'm sure you're already at the club."

"Stop apologizing. Let's meet tomorrow so

today you can concentrate on your cow. Same time, same place."

"Thanks a lot. Gotta run."

As Lila gathered her things, Sam entered. He usually dressed casually, but this morning he was in a navy suit and tie, a snowy dress shirt and black boots, a man who would turn female heads anywhere. Just the sight of him made her heart race.

"Good afternoon—looks as if you're leaving."

"I was going to meet Shannon, but she's called and canceled. She has a cow having difficulty giving birth, plus her foreman is sick."

"I'll bet you had planned to have lunch with Shannon. Now you don't have to miss the treat of dining here at the club. I'll take you to lunch."

"You know, I eat here plenty with my family," she said, amused because Sam knew full well she was frequently at the club when she was in town.

His grin widened. "I promise I'll hide my usual chauvinistic self and we'll have a good time."

"I'll have to admit, to hear you confess that you are fully aware of your old-fashioned, chauvinistic ways is refreshing."

"Come on. You were going to eat here with Shannon. You can eat with me. We can even talk about the children's center if you want."

"Now you're stretching your credibility. There's no way you have an interest in the child-care center, so don't even pretend you do."

"Didn't say I'd pretend. I just said we can discuss it—you talk and I'll listen. Let me take your things and we can leave them with the maître d'."

"You're persistent, Sam."

"Only when it's important—I'm interested and the best-looking woman in Royal, Texas, is back in town," he said, taking her things from her.

She shook her head, more at herself than at him, yet he was so tempting. What happened to her backbone where Sam was concerned? Right now she should be saying no firmly and walking out instead of watching him tuck her papers and plans beneath his arm and smile at her.

"I'm glad we're having lunch together," he said in a husky voice that sounded more like an invitation to step into his bedroom. "Now tell me about the children's center," he said, taking her arm and heading toward the door.

She had to either go along to lunch with him or make an issue of refusing now. It was much easier to just go with him because his sexy voice and spellbinding eyes had sealed the deal for him.

"They're moving ahead rapidly because Shannon and the other women have coordinated with the construction company. I'm surprised Gordon Construction didn't have the bid."

"No, we're closely involved at the TCC and felt it was a conflict of interest. This is not our deal."

"Does that translate into 'We wouldn't touch the child-care center with a ten-foot pole'?"

He grinned at her. "Sugar, you do have the wrong view of me."

"Has it ever occurred to you that your *sugar* endearment is a little demeaning?"

"*Sugar?* When applied to you? Ahh, never, Lila," he said, pausing and turning to face her, making her stop. He stood too close, looked at her too intently and had his hand on her wrist, where he could easily feel her racing pulse.

"*Sugar* where you're concerned is definitely an endearment," he said softly, bending his knees to look a little more directly into her eyes. "There is absolutely nothing demeaning about it."

"It sort of has the connotation of relegating me to the kitchen and bedroom. Have you thought about that?"

"Not at all, because that is not what I'm implying. Believe me, it is a term of endearment for someone who is very special and very female and important to me," he said in that same husky tone that made her feel as if she were on the verge of melting.

"This lunch is getting personal."

"Doesn't have to," he said cheerfully, taking her arm again and heading for the dining room.

"What are you doing here today?" she asked.

"I met a client. We're going to build a clinic for him and we met this morning for coffee and to talk about what he wants and for him to sign an agreement. It was all business, but this is a good place to bring clients."

"I agree with that, and my dad has made a few deals here himself, although he usually makes them out in the open looking at land, or at barns at cattle sales," she said, thankful to be on a safe, impersonal subject that would have no impact on their lives.

They entered the dining room and she waited while Sam talked to the maître d'. As soon as the waiter had poured their water, he left menus in their hands. It took her only minutes to make a selection from the familiar menu.

"What would you like, Lila?"

"I've got my choice in mind. What are you having?" she asked, determined that Sam would not order for her, knowing from past experiences that he expected to. She decided that if she behaved as independently as possible, maybe no more lunch offers would torment her.

"My usual lunch burger. I'm a burger guy and the club's are mouthwatering," he said, "but not as much as some other mouthwatering things in life."

"So what's your favorite burger on this menu?" she asked, trying to ignore his flirting, remembering how it had felt to run her fingers through his thick light brown hair that he wore collar length.

"The Swiss mushroom—gooey and delicious. I'll even give you a bite unless that's what you're ordering."

"Of course not. You and I are poles apart in everything, and that includes lunch items," she said, smiling at him. "Let me guess—you drink iced tea with your lunch."

"You're right, but you know that from being with me when we ate lunch together on my patio after the best night of my life."

"Wow, did I bring that one on myself. Want to hear one of the best nights of my life?" she said in a sultry tone, leaning closer toward him, although the table was large enough to keep a generous space between them.

"Of course, and how I hope it's the same night I had."

"Sorry to disappoint you. It was when I learned that a movie in which I had done the setup for the scenes had used nearly all my suggestions. It was exhilarating to know they were impressed by what I'd done, actually using most of it."

"Congratulations. That's impressive."

The waiter appeared to take their orders and looked expectantly at Lila.

"I'll have the Caesar salad, no chicken, and just my water. Mr. Gordon will have the mushroom-

and-Swiss burger, meat medium, with iced tea and shoestrings. Just put all this on my family check—Hacket," she said, and smiled at the waiter.

"Yes, Miss Hacket," he said, glancing at Sam. "Anything else?"

"Yes, there is something else. You put all that on my bill. I insist. I invited Miss Hacket to have lunch with me," Sam said in a commanding voice that caused their waiter to start writing in his tablet.

"Yes, sir."

"You even got how I like the meat cooked right," Sam said, looking amused.

"I figured you for the macho type who wants red in his meat," she said, certain she had annoyed him by ordering.

"Trying to get me in bad with your dad when he sees the club bill, or were you trying to show me how it feels when I order for you, the independent woman?" Sam asked.

"Not one thought crossed my mind about Dad, and I don't think your name would have shown up on the final bill to him. No, it was more to let you see how it feels to have someone order for you once you're over five years old and can read."

"Or maybe you have a chip on your shoulder about being the 'independent woman.'" He leaned across the table, taking her hand. "Well, sweetie, you can just order away. I'll remember your preference after this," he said in his husky, seductive voice while holding her hand and running his thumb back and forth across her knuckles, causing tingles. "I do not want to do one thing to make you unhappy or make you feel less than the very desirable, intelligent woman you are. Now, your danged independence is sort of like a cocklebur in my boot, but there are moments when you lose that independence and that's worth putting up with all the rest," he said, dropping back into the sexy tone that kept her heart racing.

He was causing the whole process of ordering for him to backfire, because this was not the result she had intended.

"Sam," she said, withdrawing her hand. "People will see you holding my hand and think we're a couple."

"And…that's so terrible?"

She smiled broadly, wishing she could make light of what he was saying as she extricated her hand. He leaned back, looking satisfied, as if he had just won the latest skirmish between them. Why had she let him cajole her into this lunch?

"In the first place, we're not a couple. In the second, I don't want to have to answer a bunch of unnecessary questions."

"We could be—it's all right with me. And questions are easy. Just yes or no will cover it, I think."

"Well, maybe if you hold the hand of every woman you dine with, people would accept a flat yes or no. So you and your brother didn't want any part of the child-care center for your business?"

"That isn't exactly what I said and that's an abrupt change in our conversation."

"Yes, it is, because we were getting up close and personal. Too personal. We're at lunch at the club. Everything I do here goes straight back to Dad."

"First of all, your dad and I are good friends. Second of all, he'll be more than happy for you to socialize with club members and you know it. Besides, all we're doing is having a friendly chat over lunch. That's as harmless as it gets."

She smiled at him. "True, Sam. It is completely meaningless as well. So who's the latest woman in your life? It has to be someone I know." Lila sipped her water and glanced around the club, hoping she'd convinced Sam that she felt the lunch was harmless and meaningless to her but suspecting she had not in the least.

When the silence stretched a little too long, she glanced at him and was startled to find him sitting back, his head tilted while he studied her. There was an intent look in his eyes and she was glad the table hid the sight of her waist from him.

"There's no woman in my life now," he answered evenly. "But I'd like for there to be a very special one and I don't need to tell you who. You know full well."

"That is so impossible."

"There's nothing impossible about it."

"I've already told you. Don't you listen? We're way too opposite. We have whole opposing philosophies—very basic differences that aren't going to change for either one of us."

"Go to dinner with me tonight. I'll take you dancing and I'll prove to you that we don't have a hill of beans' worth of differences between us that matter."

"Thank you, I already have plans. What are you doing now? What are you constructing, Sam?"

"I'm attempting to develop a relationship with a very beautiful, very reluctant woman," he said, leaning toward her, but the table and their lunches kept them apart. "Only that reluctance appears to me to be just skin-deep, Lila. I'll find out why or get past it. Is there a guy in California?"

"I don't want to go into that," she replied, eating her salad. "Your burger is getting cold."

"Aha, that's a no," he said with satisfaction.

"You don't know any such thing," she said, thinking Sam had expressive eyes that could convey all sorts of emotions. Her attention shifted to his mouth, remembering his kisses, until she realized what she was doing. Her gaze flew up to meet his and saw the mocking satisfaction in the blue depths.

She turned her attention to her salad. There was no way to stop the blush she felt in her face. "This lunch is not exactly turning out like I expected."

"You want me to back off?" he asked, still

sounding amused. "Tell me about this movie shoot you're getting ready for."

"It has a Western setting although it's contemporary and there are some ranches around here that should be perfect for various scenes. As much as possible, we'll get set up and ready before the cast comes."

"Makes me wish I had a ranch."

"In its own way, this is interesting country and the small towns have their own ambience."

"They have that, all right. Wait until a dust storm blows through."

"No, thanks. A dust storm isn't needed for this movie, so we'll pass on the dust."

"Can anyone come watch the filming?"

"There will be a place for the public, but to get up close and for some scenes, you'll have to have an invitation. Do you want me to get you one?"

"No, thanks. I can pass on that deal. Has anyone in this movie ever ridden a horse?"

"I'm sure they have."

"Tell me about this fascinating job you have. Just what do you do? Arrange furniture on a set?"

She laughed. "Sometimes, but a little more than

that. I need to help impart the film's theme and feeling through the props that we use. The set designs create atmosphere. Location is vital. I look at sites. I oversee the right props, the art department. Sometimes we can find the props we want. Sometimes we have to make our own. It's interesting, challenging, lots of thinking on your feet, so each assignment is different because each film is different."

"I can see where that would be interesting. What about the sexy movie guys?"

"They're just people."

"You say that like you mean it. I'd think any female would be attracted."

"They're larger than life on-screen and in those stories. Away from that, they're just people like everyone else."

"I'm glad you feel that way. You like being home again?"

"Of course I do."

"If you got a job in Midland and worked there, you'd be home a lot but still away."

"I don't believe they make many movies in Midland."

"I guess they don't," he said, giving her a thoughtful look that made her want to get away from his scrutiny.

She finished all she could eat of her salad, leaving half, and she noticed Sam only ate half his burger. The waiter went straight to Sam to sign for the meal.

"Thanks for the lunch, Sam." As she stood, he did, coming around to pull out her chair. He followed her to the lobby. "I'm going home now."

"Can't talk you into dinner tonight?"

She shook her head. "Sorry, I do have plans. Thanks again for lunch," she said.

"I'll walk you to your car." He fell into step beside her, taking the plans and papers from her hand.

"Have they heard anything more about Alex?" she asked.

"Not that I know about. Nathan still hasn't let the media know about the truck, but since he told the club and other people were at the scene, I think the word has gone through a segment of the Royal population."

"I'm sure it has. Sophie is still working in his

office, so I hope she's safe. I hope Nathan is keeping an eye on the office."

"I'd guess he is. Sophie should be okay. She wasn't deeply involved with Alex except through her job."

Lila paused beside a dark blue four-door car. "Thanks again."

"You have a new car?"

"Oh, no. This is just one of Dad's that I'm using while I'm here." She climbed in, then started the car. When she lowered the window, Sam folded his arms on the window's edge and bent down to talk.

"Lunch was fun. It would be a lot more fun to have dinner. I'll try again."

"Give it up, Sam. We're both better off," she said, her words becoming breathless. Now he was only inches away, his face thrust into the open window. She gazed into thickly lashed blue eyes that could immobilize her, and take her breath.

He leaned closer. "See, Lila," he said softly, "you're responding to me now. Sparks fly between us. If I felt your pulse, my guess is that it's racing," he said in a husky voice. "I'll tell you something—my pulse is racing, too. I feel what you're feeling."

"Doesn't matter, Sam," she whispered. "Nothing will come of it. Now you need to move away." He slipped his hand into the car, reaching behind her head to pull her the last few inches, and he leaned in, his mouth covering hers to kiss her.

Four

Lila's heart pounded when she drove out of the lot. She let out her breath. Her palms were damp. She was breathless from his kiss, which had set her heart racing. Her lips tingled and a pang struck her. If only Sam didn't have old-fashioned ideas. He was fun and sometimes she couldn't resist him.

As days passed, her figure was changing—her waistline was thicker. She couldn't wear her belts fastened in the notch she had once used.

She was running the risk of Sam noticing and she had to stop accepting his invitations. How was she ever going to tell him about his baby?

* * *

Sam stood a moment, watching her drive away. He ached to hold Lila. His lips still flamed from the brief, light kiss that only made him want so much more.

Why was she avoiding him? She had gone to lunch, but if he hadn't been persistent, she wouldn't have, and she turned him down flatly for dinner. Yet she responded to him. Her pulse had raced when he had touched her wrist. There had to be a reason for the contradictions in her.

When he was at the club now, he couldn't keep from going by the billiard room and looking for her. During lunch she had challenged him, making a pointed effort to emphasize their differences, yet at the same time she had been as responsive physically as ever. The look she'd had when he had caught her gazing at his mouth practically screamed that she wanted to kiss. So why was she refusing to go out with him?

He couldn't believe it was simply the differences in their views regarding women and the children's center. Her reasons to avoid him went deeper, but he was at a loss.

One thing he knew for sure—he wanted her in his arms. He wanted to hold and kiss her and make love for hours. Why couldn't he get her out of his system?

He returned to his office, heading down the drive to the two-story red-brick Greek Revival with stately white Corinthian columns and a broad porch flanked by well-tended beds of flowers in the front. He spent a few minutes talking to Josh and then shut himself in his big office. After half an hour he tossed down the pen he held. Why was Lila trying to avoid him? She seemed torn between responding to him and turning his every invitation down. When he had coaxed her into accepting lunch, her reluctance had been evident.

If she didn't have that other side to her, he would leave her alone and make a bigger effort to get her out of his system. As it was, he wanted to know why. And he wanted a long weekend with her where they could make love like before.

Was there a man in California?

Sam leaned back in his chair and rubbed his forehead. He didn't think so. She would be firmer in her refusals and he guessed Lila was open enough to just tell him if there was someone else. So what the hell was it? He scratched his head and sighed, standing and moving restlessly to the window.

He needed to go out with her and learn what the problem between them was or just forget her. But forgetting her was impossible. He thought about her constantly. One more night with her and maybe he could get her out of his system. Only he knew better. One night would never shake Lila out of his thoughts. He wanted unending nights.

How was he going to get even a single night with her when she was so standoffish?

He decided to go see how the latest house was progressing. He had a contract to build a seven-million-dollar mansion in Pine Valley, where he lived. He had to get out and do something to take his mind off Lila.

On Thursday, Lila showered to get ready to once again drive to Royal to meet Shannon. Tired of wearing the waist-hiding dresses, she pulled on scarlet slacks with a matching short-sleeved V-neck summer sweater. When she studied her image, she could see a small bulge. Her waist was thickening already. The clubhouse would be air-conditioned, so she pulled out a short-sleeved lightweight cardigan that matched her outfit and put it on.

This time when she looked in the mirror, she was satisfied with her image. Combing her hair, she let it fall loose. She picked up her purse, notebook and the mailing tube with the plans and drawings inside.

When she entered the present billiard room, Shannon was there along with some of the other women. Lila greeted Abby Price, Missy Reynolds and Vanessa Woodrow. In minutes they were all seated around a table, studying each other's written suggestions.

Within the hour, they moved to the dining room to continue planning over lunch. As they finished eating and lingered over iced tea, still talking about the center, Lila felt a prickle of awareness. Glancing around, she saw Sam standing in the doorway. Her heart skipped a beat when he turned to look at her. For a moment she was locked into his gaze until she realized she was staring.

With an effort she looked away, focusing again on the women at her table and trying to ignore Sam.

Moments later, when she couldn't resist glancing toward the door, he had disappeared from sight. She suspected she would see him later. He had a way of popping up when she least expected to see him.

When the women adjourned to the billiard room again, everyone shared a few final ideas. They wanted bright and colorful play areas and a separate corner for babies.

Shannon looked at her list. "We'll have security cameras and parents will be able to access a closed-circuit view of the center so they can see their child."

"We'll have security at the front door and alarms will sound if anyone opens any of the doors except the front, which has a chime if opened, but two people will be at the desk by the front door at all times," Missy added.

Later, after the others had gone, only Shannon and Lila were left. As Lila put away her notes, she paused. "I think this child-care center is going to be great. The designs we have are bright and appealing."

"Thanks for your input. The California shop you told us about where we can get pictures for the walls is wonderful."

"I'm glad all of you found it helpful. I love to go there and see what they have when I need to get a shower gift or new-baby present."

"We're getting more support, even from some of the members who opposed this center."

"But still not the Gordons."

"Heavens, no. Both Gordons fought this like crazy. Frankly, so did your dad. Some people don't change."

"I know my dad doesn't change and Hack is going to be like him, only worse. But my mom is enthusiastic about the center. Her ladies' book club is making a donation and I think Mom made a big donation herself. Dad will never know she had a part in it," Lila said, laughing.

"Good for her. We want the best possible place for the children. We barely touched on it today, but our budget is maxed out. That's something else we'll have to tackle."

"I'm sure we can get more money."

"Lila, if we need to get together again, I'll give you a call."

"Sure, but when I go back to work, I can't meet with you."

"I understand. Soon I'll be leaving for Austin. I'm ready to see Rory," Shannon said wistfully.

"Bye, Shannon," Lila said as her friend left. Gathering the rest of her things, Lila remembered her mother was in Midland with friends and wouldn't be home until later. Her dad was with her uncle in Houston to look at a bull. She didn't want to go home and listen to Hack, or worse, have to put up with Hack and some of his friends. As Lila walked toward the door, she paused to look at the room. Half of the old billiard tables were scheduled to be removed while half would remain. Renovations would start as soon as the center was finished. The clubhouse was getting updated continually, yet still retained some of its historic parts.

"Taking a last look at this room before they start working on it?" came a deep male voice, and she turned to see Sam strolling into the room. "I just passed Shannon and she said you're through for today."

"That's right."

Sam stopped inches in front of her. He stood too close and her heartbeat raced.

"Come have a drink with me. We can sit on the terrace or we can stay in the air-conditioned bar."

Lila debated a moment.

"I take that as a definite yes," Sam said, taking her notebook from her hands. "I'll carry this."

"You're sure of yourself," she said, her gaze raking over him as he turned. His short-sleeved navy Western shirt had the top two buttons unfastened. Wearing tight jeans and boots, he looked as if he had just come from a ranch, but Lila knew Sam dressed like the ranchers most of the time, she guessed because he worked with so many of them and had grown up on a ranch.

"You don't have something else you have to do and you don't look in a hurry to head home."

"Now, how do you know all that? You're guessing," she said, smiling, knowing she was once again yielding to Sam when she should have said no and gotten away from him as quickly as possible. "I was just thinking that Mom's in Midland until later. Dad's in Houston with my uncle. My little brother will be as eager to spend time with me as I am with him," she said dryly. "Hack is at an age that is not the most adorable time."

"So I'm the lucky guy who gets your company—I knew there was a reason I came by the club. How's the children's center coming along?" Sam asked, walking around the room and looking at the racks holding cue sticks, the tables with the balls ready.

"We've got all sorts of plans and the renovation of the old billiard room is progressing faster than I dreamed possible."

"Good."

"I'm surprised to hear you say that," she said.

"It's a done deal, so I might as well accept it."

"That's a good attitude," she said, wondering how much he meant what he said.

"Do you know how to shoot pool?"

"Yes, I do."

"Want to play? I can give you some points."

"I'll play and you don't have to give me any

points," she said, wondering why they constantly challenged each other.

He smiled and got cue sticks, handing her one. He racked the balls.

"You can start," he said. "Go ahead and bust them."

"Sure," she said. As she lined up her shot, she concentrated, determined to beat him.

"Many a game has been played on these tables and many a deal done while the game went on," he said when it was his turn.

"Deals have been done all over this clubhouse. It would be interesting to hear what the highest amount involved was. My guess is it was in the millions but not billions."

"I agree. I doubt if a billion-dollar deal went down here at the clubhouse, but we both might be wrong. And other kinds of deals have been done. Seductions, marriage proposals, clandestine meetings, probably divorce lawyers meeting with clients here. Wagers that involved all sorts of things. Will you wager on our game?"

He straightened to watch his shot, then looked at her before he moved to shoot again.

"Maybe. If I lose, what does it cost me?"

He shot and balls rolled away. "All right. If I win," he said, straightening to look into her eyes as she realized she should have refused the bet, "I get a kiss."

A tingle slithered to her toes. "Only a kiss," she said as if his kisses didn't set her on fire. "Okay." Instantly she knew what she wanted. "If I win, you make a contribution to the child-care center," she said, resolving to get a donation for the center and avoid a kiss that would incinerate her. "It has to be over fifty dollars."

"You're on," he replied, smiling at her.

She focused on the game and for the next few minutes they played in silence, evenly matched, but she was concentrating and trying to play her best.

And then she missed a shot. Holding her breath, she watched as he made his. In minutes the game was his.

He came around to take her cue stick and put it in the rack next to his. While her heart drummed, she watched his every move.

He turned back and his blue eyes held smoldering fires. He walked to her and slipped his arm around her waist. "To the victor...and all that," he said. His gaze lowered to her mouth and her lips tingled in anticipation.

He bent lower, slowly, tantalizingly, and then his lips brushed hers. The next time, his mouth touched hers with pressure, opening her mouth, and desire swept her. She melted against him, winding her arm around his neck, returning his kiss as his tongue went deep into her mouth. Moaning softly, she was barely aware she had made a sound.

Burning with need, she ran her fingers in his hair. Why? Why did he hold such appeal for her when they were so vastly different?

His kiss continued and time ceased to exist. She kissed him in return while she wanted the barriers between them gone. She wanted more, ached for hours of loving that they'd had once before.

When she ended the kiss, she was breathless, looking up at him as she stepped away.

"Want a second match?" he asked lightly, but his voice was hoarse and his breathing ragged.

"No, I think not."

He took her hand. "Maybe later. C'mon. We'll go to the bar and have a cool drink where we can talk."

A few minutes later they were seated in a booth in the bar among only a half-dozen members. Soft music played and a waiter appeared to take their order. "Ginger ale for me," Lila said.

"Beer, chips and *queso*," Sam ordered. "Ginger ale?" he asked when the waiter was gone.

"That's all I feel like and I have to drive back to the ranch tonight."

"No, you don't," Sam said, folding his arms on the table to lean closer. "I'll be glad to take you home. Or, even better—"

"Don't say it," she said, smiling at him. "I'm definitely going home tonight."

"But not for a while. We can have some fun before you do. How did you get this job that you like so much? Is that what you went to Hollywood to do?"

"Yes, but I started much lower and when that job came open, I applied and interviewed for it along with quite a few others." As she talked, he listened as if totally entranced. She gazed at him and thought he had the bluest eyes she had ever seen. She worked with movie stars, men who were considered by millions to be handsome and sexy, and she had never had the reaction to any of them she had by simply being near Sam. That bit of knowledge annoyed her as much as it mystified her.

They talked, laughing over things that had happened in Royal. She lost track of time, but when a pianist began to play, she glanced around in surprise and looked at her watch.

Sam's hand closed on her wrist, hiding her watch. "It's time for dinner, maybe a dance with you. It's still early. We can eat here in the bar."

He motioned to their waiter and asked for menus.

"You can't keep from taking charge, can you?"

"You surely can't object to that."

"Of course not. It's just amusing because it's ingrained in you. With a twin brother, there must have been some fights and competition. I'm guessing Josh may be as take-charge as you."

Sam gave her a look that made her realize she was right and might have touched a nerve. "We had fights plenty. Big fights. And we are competitive. But we also stood up for each other. We can work together well and the business has been a good thing."

"That's great, Sam. I don't know about any of that. Hack is younger. When he was a toddler, I thought he was so cute. He was my doll, and I helped Mom with him. Dad spoils him. Mom's aware of it and has tried to get Dad to be more firm with Hack, but he isn't. A time came when Hack was no longer a baby and not so cute. We fought like cats and dogs all the way through school until I went off to college. Now he's just a nuisance sometimes or we leave each other alone. It's sad. We've grown apart and I don't think that's going to change. The one person Hack is really nice to is Mom, but he does things behind her back that he knows she doesn't want him to do. I don't know if we'll ever be close and I can't imagine ever being in a business with Hack."

"I will have to agree with you that your little brother is one spoiled kid."

"I hope he matures and changes and begins to care about someone besides himself. Enough about him, though. Families are a big influence in our lives. I'm sorry you lost your mom when you were so young. I'm close to mine."

"Yeah. Life throws us curves. What would you like to eat?"

She studied the menu even though she was not really hungry. "I think just a spinach salad."

"You can do better than that. Let's dance and maybe you'll work up an appetite."

She went with him to the dance floor and soon they were turning to a fast beat, moving with the music. Sam was a good dancer, light on his feet, moving in a sensual way while he watched her with a steady, smoldering gaze.

Each time with him was a mistake, yet she kept accepting his invitations. Soon she'd be busy with the movie and then she'd head back to California and Sam would be a memory again. Except she had to tell him the truth. When was the time going to be right?

Twisting and turning, her feet moved in rhythm. The time was definitely not now. Not until it was almost time to go back to California. Two or three days before, so he could get some things out of his system while she was still around. Afterward she would go to California, and he would have to adjust to the idea.

They danced three fast numbers before there was a ballad. Along with the music, the piano player sang a sentimental love song. Sam wrapped her in his embrace, pulling her close to slow-dance with her.

Why did it feel so right to be in his arms? To sway with him, feel his solid muscles against her? The slow steps and being held close revved desire, making her think of lovemaking with him.

When the number ended, she looked up and saw the need mirrored in the depths of his eyes. "I want you, Lila," he whispered. "I want to make love again."

"Sam," she cautioned, shaking her head. "Let's get off the dance floor," she whispered. She felt as if all her resolve was melting away. "Now I'm ready for dinner," she said, struggling to change the subject.

She wasn't one degree more hungry than she had been before, but the dancing was too close, too personal. They were touching, hugging, making sexy moves in the fast dances. She wanted to get back to the booth with a table between them, have dinner and then drive herself home. The evening had been fun, but she needed to keep him at arm's length and end it early.

Their waiter appeared, refilling their glasses before asking what she wanted.

"The spinach salad," she said.

"Is that all? You'll be hungry before you get home," Sam said.

She shook her head. "That's all."

"I'll have the New York strip, cooked medium," Sam said.

She slid out of the booth. "Need to freshen up," she said. As she walked away, her back tingled and she felt Sam's gaze on her.

In the lobby she stopped to call home because her mother worried if she didn't know where her children were.

As wild as her brother was, he kept his mother fairly well informed about where he would be. That was one of the few considerations Hack gave anyone.

No one answered at the Double H. Lila left a message because her mother checked when she returned home.

* * *

Sam watched Lila as she crossed the room. When he'd held her close, she had felt different than last time. Her waist wasn't as tiny as he had remembered. She was still soft curves, warm, enticing. He wanted her and he wanted to talk her into staying in Pine Valley at his house tonight.

When she returned, he watched her approach the table. He stood, waiting until she was seated before he sat again. He wondered whether she really disliked all the old-time courtesies or just certain ones, like ordering for her.

She was too damned independent, yet he just couldn't get her out of his system. He thought there was only one way to do so—make love until he was totally satisfied and could walk away without looking back.

Trouble was, the lady wasn't cooperating. He wasn't getting any chances for lovemaking, but tonight he was making inroads on her resistance.

As they ate, they talked about various topics. She took dainty bites, dawdling over her salad as if she didn't really want it.

Finally they finished, and when they returned to the dance floor for a fast, pounding song, he watched her with growing desire. She had pulled off the cardigan she wore over her short-sleeved scarlet sweater. Lights had dimmed and it was darker than it had been earlier.

She danced around him, hips moving. Strobe lights flashed and the dance floor filled with other dancers, everyone gyrating to the loud music.

Lights slashed across them, flashing on her face and then plunging her into darkness. Lights showed her green eyes, her flushed cheeks, the dark auburn hair swirling out behind her when she spun around. More streaks of light cut across the V of her sweater, revealing her lush curves and creamy skin. The next flash and his gaze was on her waist and stomach. He was startled to see her tummy looked slightly rounded, not flat below her tiny waist as before. The light was gone instantly. The next flash she had turned away.

He broke into a sweat as he danced, while she looked cool, composed. He wanted her more than ever.

The dance ended with a crash of drums and

then a ballad started and he pulled her into his arms to hold her close and barely move in time to the music.

They danced in silence, but this time he thought about her and felt her soft body pressed against him. He ran his hand down over her hip, back up until he reached her ribs and she caught his wrist and moved his hand to her back.

She was thicker through the middle, her stomach a bit fuller, not the flat stomach she'd had before. He thought about the cardigan she had worn throughout the hot day, yet in the air-conditioned club, it would not be unpleasant to wear.

He pictured her as she had looked at the barbecue, remembering her dress and how it had hidden her waist. So had the dresses he had seen her wear at the club. Everything until today, and even then, the cardigan hid her waist fairly well.

Sam tightened his arm to pull her closer, wondering if she felt so different or if his memory wasn't good. A weight gain? He thought of how she avoided him, usually wouldn't go out with him, turning him down. Yet at the same time, she had a response every time he was around, as if she wanted him but shouldn't.

One possibility occurred to him, sending such a shock through his body that he stopped dancing.

Five

Sam quickly regained his composure. He counted back and realized it was a full three months since their night together.

He felt as if all the breath had been knocked out of him. Lila was going to have a baby—his baby. He was as sure of it as he was that flowers would grow in the spring. That would explain her contradictory actions, one minute flirting and the next throwing an invisible wall between them and refusing to go out with him.

He would be a dad. Lila was going to have his baby. He felt weak in the knees, as if he'd had a major blow to his middle.

Had she come to Texas and expected to avoid telling him? Anger stirred that she would hide from him the truth about his baby. Maybe she was going to wait until she was back in California to let him know. She had to know she couldn't hide it forever. She obviously intended to keep the baby or she would have already done something. That thought gave him chills.

A baby. Their baby. Stunned, he danced automatically, forgetting everyone around him. He would have to marry her.

The moment that occurred to him, he felt another blow to his insides that took his breath. Get married. His first reaction was a panicky feeling of being trapped.

As quickly as he'd thought of marriage, he focused on Lila. His panicky feelings evaporated. Lila was beautiful, intelligent, sexy. Marriage to Lila, a family of his own, life couldn't get any better. She was also totally independent, the epitome of the independent woman. Lila would not want to marry—if she did, she would not have been trying to avoid him.

The dance ended and another started. Without

a word, he began to dance and she followed his lead, another fast piece where they danced with space between them and he could watch her and think and adjust to his discovery.

His baby. That was a miracle. His own family—if he could ever convince her to marry him.

It astounded him and annoyed him that she wouldn't share the news with him. He wanted to sweep her up and lift her high, showering kisses on her. He was going to marry Lila. He was going to be a dad.

An old favorite started playing and he drew her into his arms for some close dancing. "This is good, Lila," he said in a husky voice, his mind wrapped up in his new discovery. "Let me take you to dinner tomorrow night."

He whirled her around and dipped, pausing. As she gazed up into his eyes, her arm tightened around his neck, making his heart pound. He wanted to kiss her full, rosy lips. He tightened his arms as she wound her fingers in the hair at the back of his head.

"Sam," she whispered.

Their gazes locked and he forgot the other dancers. He wanted her more than he ever had before. This would be good, he decided. Good, when—and if—he could talk her into marriage.

"We'll go to dinner and celebrate the new movie and talk. I'll pick you up at six," he said, slowly straightening and taking her up with him while their gazes still held.

When he looked at her mouth, she licked her lower lip. His body tensed, heated with desire. He pulled her closer to continue dancing while he looked into her green eyes. "We'll go to my place and I'll cook my special steaks. How's that?"

"Sam—"

"It's Friday night. You want to stay out at the ranch with Hack?"

She smiled. "I think on Friday night the last place Hack will be is at the Double H."

"I'll pick you up at six, darlin'. You'll have a fun evening and I can show you my new outdoor kitchen and cook you the best steak west of the Mississippi. How's that for an offer you can't refuse? I might even throw in taking you dancing later."

"You're impossible," she said, smiling.

"But oh so interested in the beautiful lady and wanting to spend an evening together. We might even shoot another game of pool with another wager. I'll give you a chance to win that donation to the child center yet."

"Even if I won, I don't think you'd keep your promise on a donation to the child-care center."

"I'm not that opposed to the little tykes. You misjudge me. You doubt my word?"

"Please, Sam, I've heard you talk and I know exactly how you feel about them. I've heard how you and your brother really campaigned against the center. An evening together—all we'll do is fuss and fight."

"Absolutely not! There will be nothing but harmony—well, maybe a challenge or two—tomorrow night."

"Why do I think that's the understatement of this century?" she asked, laughing.

"There, I made you laugh. That's the best, Lila. When you laugh, you light up and I love it. I'll have to try harder."

He fought the urge to let his eyes roam over her waist. Instead, he walked beside her, asking her if she wanted anything to drink. When she chose a glass of lemonade, he summoned a waiter and placed an order for lemonade and for another cold bottle of beer.

As she stood beside her chair, his gaze slipped over her. There was the slightest bulge to her tummy. A bulge she definitely had not had three months earlier.

While he held her chair, his fingers played across her nape. He wanted to pull her to her feet and ask her about the pregnancy, but this wasn't the time or place.

As soon as their drinks arrived, she excused herself, picked up her purse and headed for the ladies' room.

Still in shock, he watched her walk away. He would have to talk her into marriage. He was certain she had already made up her mind to be a single mom. Not with his baby, would she be. He could be determined, too, and he wasn't going to let her independence mess up their child's life.

Lila went to the ladies' room and studied her image. Thank goodness the club had the lights dimmed in the dining room, although she thought her slacks and sweater hid her figure well enough. Most men she had known were not keenly observant. Heaven knows, the men in her family weren't.

She returned to the table to face Sam, who sat across from her. He looked relaxed, yet she had the feeling he was studying her intently all through their light conversation.

"When they start shooting a movie here, it'll turn this town upside down."

"Like I said, so far there's no indication it will be in Royal. Or even in Maverick County. And if something changes and a scene is shot here, I think most people are level-headed. Sam, it's time for me to start home."

He motioned for the tab and then she picked up her purse. In the foyer, he collected her things.

"We could go out to my house," he suggested. "You can stay there and it'll save you a drive this late. Or leave your car here at the club. I'll take you home."

"It's not that late."

"If you're going to go, I insist on driving."

"Just how helpless do you think I am?" she asked, annoyed and amused at the same time.

"Not helpless at all. That's not the point. Maybe I want to be with you a little longer—ever think of that?"

"All right," she said, suspecting she would lose the argument no matter how long they debated. Sam had a stubborn lift to his chin. "I'll leave my car here and you can drive me home."

"Great." He took her arm and they walked out to his sleek black sports car. Sam held the door and she slid onto the soft leather seat.

As he walked around the car, her gaze ran over him and she thought about dancing with him when he held her close. Now she was going to dinner with him tomorrow night. Would she ever be able to stop letting him talk her into things?

He slid behind the wheel, glancing at her when he drove away from the club. "What do you do for entertainment in California?"

"That's easy. Go to the beach. I love the ocean. It's exciting, awesome, wonderful. I walk on the beach every day. I swim a lot of the time." She turned in the seat to face him. The lights from the dash highlighted his prominent cheekbones, the bulge of his biceps.

Would he kiss her good-night? Her anticipation blossomed, spreading heat low within her.

During the drive he kept her entertained with conversation and when he circled in front of the Double H, he parked at the foot of the front steps.

He came around to walk her to the door. "It was a fun evening, Sam," she said as she crossed the porch and stopped in front of the entranceway.

"I hope so, because it was for me," he said, brushing his hand lightly on her cheek. "Do you think your family is home?"

"I'm sure my parents are and have gone to bed. It doesn't matter. I have a key so I can get in."

He smiled. "I'll see you tomorrow night at six." He walked away and she turned to go inside. For an instant, even though she knew she shouldn't, she felt a flash of disappointment that he hadn't kissed her. She could still feel the brush of his hand on her cheek, a touching caress that seemed uncharacteristic of the Sam she knew.

She had to tell him the truth about the baby, but it was important to wait until the perfect moment.

* * *

Friday evening Lila was more nervous than ever. She had changed clothes three times, finally deciding on a sleeveless blue dress. It had a straight skirt that ended above her knees. She hoped her legs would take his attention. The dress had a matching short-sleeved cardigan sweater.

She left her hair loose. She wanted him looking at her hair, her face, her legs, anywhere except her expanding middle. There was a light rap on the door and her mother entered. Dressed in casual pink slacks and a pink shirt, she reminded Lila of the mothers on sitcoms when she was a little girl. The ideal wife—in another time and another era.

"You look beautiful, Lila. Just radiant."

"I don't feel so radiant, but thank you, Mom."

"Think about it. Tonight might be a good time to tell the news to Sam," Barbara said, sitting on an upholstered blue-and-white-striped chair while she watched Lila brush her hair.

"No. I just can't do it this early in my stay. He'll hound me to pieces. I'll tell him, but in time."

"Lila, Sam's the father of your baby. I think you're too harsh on him."

Lila smiled as chimes sounded. "Here he is, and I'll be nice to him," she said, amused by her mother. "You let him in and you can talk to him a few minutes since you think he's so great."

"I'll be glad to," Barbara said, leaving the room. Lila took another long, critical look at her image in the full-length mirror and decided the dress looked fine and hid everything it needed to.

She picked up her purse and went to find Sam.

Sam stood as she entered the room.

"Come join us, Lila," her dad said. "Sam and I are talking about a golf game this weekend."

Sam barely heard Beau as his gaze swept over Lila. His heart missed a beat. She wore another sleeveless cotton dress with plain lines, yet on her the dress looked great, showing off her fabulous legs. The neckline gave a tantalizing glimpse of lush curves and her green eyes were wide, thickly lashed, holding a sexy look of approval as her gaze swept over him.

There was a current of excitement that had his nerves on edge. Tonight he wanted to know the truth and he intended to confront Lila about it.

For the next half hour they sat with her parents until Lila turned down her father's offer of drinks. Sam declined, too, rising to his feet to cross the room.

"I promised Lila dinner, so it's time we leave for Royal, but I've enjoyed seeing you both. Everyone is still talking about what a fabulous barbecue you had this year. You outdid yourselves, and the Hacket barbecue became an even bigger legend."

"It's fun to do," Barbara said, walking with them to the door.

"It was a damn fine barbecue, if I do say so myself," Beau said, smiling broadly. "Bring my baby home at a decent hour, Sam."

"Yes, sir. It's also nice to have Lila back in Texas."

"Night, Mom, Dad," she said as Sam took her arm to walk to the car. "My parents really like you, Sam."

"You have nice parents. It's another member of the family that I really want to like me," he said, flirting with her.

"He does," she said.

"I'm definitely not referring to your kid brother and you know it," he said.

"Of course I like you or I wouldn't be going out with you tonight. I consider you a very good friend of the family. The whole family."

"Well, then, I'm going to change that," he drawled in a deeper tone of voice.

"Don't make me a project."

"It might be fun, darlin'. Watch what you ask."

"You control yourself, Sam," she cautioned.

"Something that's impossible to do if I have a chance to kiss you. There's no way I can resist taking the opportunity. Maybe if we just start now, I'll get all this kissing out of my system and we can enjoy an ordinary evening."

"Nice try, but no, we're not starting with kisses. Absolutely not."

"My place tonight, later, dancing if you want," he said, holding open the door to his sports car. He looked at her shapely calves as she climbed into the car. When he looked up, he found her watching him.

They drove back to Pine Valley, the ultra-up-scale gated community where he lived. Security let him enter and the gatekeeper waved to him. He glanced at Lila to see her looking outside at drives that turned into emerald lawns covered with tall trees. Occasionally there was a glimpse of a sprawling, imposing mansion set back far from the main road.

"I hear you're constructing a new home out here."

"You heard right. Actually, more than one. I like working on houses in Pine Valley. They're big, expensive, challenging. They'll be my neighbors, so I like getting to know the owners," he said. Her perfume lingered in the air, an enticing scent that smelled of spring flowers.

As they approached his mansion, she stared at it. "It's beautiful here."

"I can stretch out and enjoy myself. I have my dream home," he said. "But you've seen my home and my bedroom already."

"So I don't need to see it tonight."

He pulled over and stopped, turning to her, sliding his arm across the back of the seat. She shifted to look at him, her green eyes opening wide. Her lush lips were a temptation and he ached to draw her into his arms and kiss her. "I'm going to find out why you're fighting me, Lila. Half of you is at war with me or wanting to avoid me, and the other half is sending me signals and still kissing me with enough heat to melt solid metal."

"I don't think so," she said breathlessly, gazing at him with seductive eyes that made his breath catch. Did she have any clue the impact she had on him?

"You're doing it now. Your eyes say yes, your body is responding, yet your words are holding me at arm's length. I'm going to find out what it is that's coming between us."

"Some things are best not disturbed, Sam. If you push, I'll disappear," she said, her words almost a whisper.

"I really am curious. I'll get an answer."

"When you do, you may wish you had left well enough alone," she said, her voice firmer.

"Now, that's interesting because that's a threat," he said, running his hand across her nape, feeling her smooth, warm skin.

"Stubborn, stubborn man. I'm not threatening

you. I think you've asked me out solely because I've said no to you a couple of times."

"More than a couple," he replied. "No, definitely not because you've said no. I've asked you out because I want to be with you and because some of the time you seem to want to be with me," he said, his voice getting softer, dropping.

"Just be careful, Sam. You're going where you don't want to go. I said yes to tonight because we had fun together and I thought this would be another fun, light evening."

"We'll try to keep it that way," he said. Knowing he should move away or he would kiss her, he leaned back, then drove around to the rear of the mansion.

Lila waited in the outdoor living area overlooking the patio and the pool while Sam got a lemonade for her and a cold beer for himself. She sat on one end of a sofa covered in a colorful fabric patterned with red tulips.

She watched Sam getting their drinks. He paused to shed the navy sport coat he wore and rolled up the sleeves of the pale blue cotton shirt that was tucked into navy slacks. As always, he wore Western boots. Classical music played softly in the background. She had a pang of longing, wishing that everything was all right between them, and this was just an evening out with him.

She stopped thinking about wishes and faced the reality that soon she would have to tell him about his baby.

"This is good, Lila," he said, sitting close beside her on the sofa.

Intensely aware of him, she smiled. "It will never be really good between us, because we're from different worlds. You're part of another century, with old-fashioned ideas—"

"Old-fashioned ideas aren't always bad. I have one right now. I'll show you one that is really old-fashioned," he said softly, closing the distance between them as his gaze went to her mouth.

Sam took her lemonade from her hands and set it on the table, placing his beer beside it.

Her insides tightened and she inhaled. "Sam—" she whispered, a protest that died the instant his lips brushed hers lightly and then settled on hers to kiss her.

Carried from a world of concern to a sensual world of desire, she closed her eyes and placed her hands on his forearms. His hand slid down her back, and his other hand caressed her nape. Kissing him in return, she ran her hands across his broad shoulders, longing for more, to freely make love, to not have to deal with their opposing views of life.

When she finally leaned back, she tried to catch her breath as she looked into his blue eyes.

"I asked you out tonight because I wanted to be with you. But I had another reason, Lila. I've noticed some things and I'm curious," he said, gazing intently at her, causing her heart to beat faster. "You're pregnant, aren't you? You're carrying my baby."

Six

Her heart missed a beat and then began to pound. For a moment she couldn't get her breath and her head spun. He leaned closer, giving her a searching look.

"You're pregnant, aren't you?"

"Yes," she admitted, her head swimming. "How did you know?"

"I figured it out." He inhaled deeply. "What were you going to do? Go back to California and not tell me? Send me a text someday?"

"No, I knew I'd have to tell you," she said, gulping for air and feeling as if she might faint.

"Are you all right?" he asked, his tone changing as he brushed her hair away from her face.

"No, I'm not all right," she snapped. "This isn't the way I wanted to tell you. How long have you known?" she asked. "I think I'm going to faint."

"Put your head down," he said, and left to return in seconds with a cold wet cloth he placed on the back of her neck.

"Lila, I don't want to upset you, but we should talk. A baby is not something you can hide for very long."

"I know that," she said, sitting up and taking the cloth to wipe her brow. She leaned back. Sam had one arm stretched on the back of the sofa and he was turned toward her, his knees touching her leg. He sat close and his gaze was still intense, as if he had never really looked at her before.

"Look, sugar, I didn't intend to make you faint," he said gently, and she thought it was so typical of him. His tone was like a squeeze to her heart, gentle, comforting, yet his endearment, *sugar,* annoyed her. How was she going to deal with him? It was the question that had plagued her since discovering her pregnancy.

"Sam, please don't call me *sugar.*"

"I meant it in a nice way. Damn, Lila, do I have to call you Ms. Hacket?"

She had to smile as she opened her eyes and looked at him. She held the wet cloth. "No, you don't ever have to call me Ms. Hacket. And yes, I'm pregnant from our night together. I'm as shocked as you must be because we took precautions."

"That wasn't so damn hard to tell me, was it?" he asked, staring solemnly at her again.

"I guess not. It's what will follow now that will be difficult. You and I are so totally different."

"Differences that are incredibly appealing to me," he said, wrapping his arms around her lightly. Nothing was going as she had expected.

They gazed into each other's eyes and her heartbeat should have been loud enough for him to hear. Below his thick brown hair, which partially fell on his wide forehead, his blue eyes were intense. Desire flared, burning brightly in their depths. He looked at her lips and her mouth went dry. Sam was too physically appealing to her. "You're my downfall, Sam Gordon," she whispered.

"Never, darlin'," he replied softly before he

kissed her again. His arms tightened and he shifted her, lifting her to his lap and cradling her against his shoulder while they kissed.

His kiss was stormy, possessive, melting her as always and igniting fires of longing. She didn't want this breathless, heart-stopping reaction to his kisses. She didn't want this wild surge of passion and this burning need for more of him. While thoughts of denial streamed in her consciousness, her body responded and she wrapped her arms around him.

When she realized how hungrily she responded, she pulled back and slipped off his lap, standing and walking away, trying to get some distance between them while she regained her poise. She turned to find him watching her. He sat on the sofa, his elbows on his knees, his blue shirt open at the throat.

He came to his feet slowly and her pulse began to drum again as she watched him approach. Determination showed in his eyes, his expression, his walk, making her brace for the battle to come. His chin had a stubborn jut to it while a muscle worked in his jaw, and he had a half-lidded stare that jangled her nerves.

Placing both hands on her shoulders, he stood quietly, studying her with a piercing gaze that was even more unnerving. Silence stretched between them.

"We can work this out," she said firmly.

"Oh, yeah, we will," he said. His self-assurance set her more on edge, making her certain he had already started planning for the baby. "Let's look through my house. Whatever happens, I'll have a nursery built because I get to see my own child."

Startled, she had never anticipated his request that was unnecessary at this time. "I'll be happy to look, but it's too early to plan a nursery."

"Maybe. Won't hurt. You can humor me on this one. It will give us a chance to get used to both of us knowing about the baby."

"I guess you're right," she replied, not caring if he wanted to start planning a nursery in his house. That was the least of her concerns. He brushed a light kiss on the corner of her mouth.

"There, that's better. I want you happy," he said,

his expression serious. She hoped he really meant what he said.

"I'll try to make you happy," he said as if he could guess her thoughts.

"Of course you will," she said, wondering what he was up to because he had become reasonable and cooperative, not his usual take-charge self, not at all what she had expected. Sam and his twin, Josh, were both strong-willed men who were accustomed to getting their way, so this sudden change in tactics had her guard up more than ever.

"Sure. I'll be happy to look with you."

"Lila, this is my baby, too. Dads have rights, too," Sam said, draping his arm across her shoulders and pulling her closer beside him.

"I know you do," she said, aware of touching him, wishing he weren't so old-fashioned yet knowing that was as ingrained in him as breathing.

"I just thought perhaps you intended to return to California and spread the word that you had a baby by some guy out there."

She stopped walking to face him and shake her head. "I wouldn't do that. I've been in shock because neither of us expected this, but I planned to tell you. I was trying to get accustomed to the idea myself before letting others know."

"Others is one thing. The father—me—is another. Does your family all know?"

"Heavens, no," she blurted before she thought. "You know Dad doesn't. Nor does Hack. I can't listen to Hack and all the remarks I'll get from him. Not yet. No. My mom knows."

"There's a way to avoid having to listen to remarks from Hack and from anyone else," Sam said quietly, creating a prickle of caution in her.

"I'm not sure I want to hear this. At least not this soon."

"Sooner is better." He took her hands, holding them lightly. "Has it ever occurred to you that you might be too independent for your own good?"

She shook her head. "That's where our views of life are so different. No, I don't think I'm too independent for my own good. I don't think I'm any different from a large percentage of the women in the U.S. Did it ever occur to you that you have very old-fashioned views of women that don't even apply to most of the women you know?"

"Seems to me there are plenty of women around here who are just as I expected."

"Maybe, or maybe they're just trying to please you because you're a nice guy," she said, trying to lighten the moment and postpone discussing their future.

He smiled. "And you don't care to try to please me?"

"Sam, you and I have 'pleased' each other enough that now we have a baby between us," she said, seeing the sparkle flash in his eyes while the corner of his mouth lifted.

"I'd almost forgotten how straightforward you can be. And it was damn fun and good, I'd say. Actually, pregnancy becomes you. You have a rosy glow and look gorgeous tonight," he added huskily.

"Thank you," she replied, feeling a degree better while thinking he looked incredibly good himself in the pale blue shirt that made his eyes look even bluer.

They walked through a wide hallway to a sweeping double staircase. The graceful stairs had a black wrought-iron railing. No stretch of her imagination could envision a child running up and down the fancy stairs.

"This is a showcase house. I can't imagine a little child running through here. These stairs are not kid friendly."

"I'll have to admit, I'm with you there. Maybe I'll have this iron railing taken out. Like you, I'm adjusting to the idea of a baby in my life."

She took a deep breath and let it out slowly, trying to relax. She could feel the tension between her shoulders. She hadn't made any decisions about her future, something she had planned to do before Sam learned of her pregnancy. Now he would want to be involved in everything.

"This nursery business—you're adjusting to the news faster than I thought you would."

He grinned. "Care to make a wager on which one of us makes the most adjustments to the way of living in the next month?"

"I'm not wagering with you over anything again," she said.

"Why not? I know you liked kissing me. Matter of fact, let me show you. I can prove it," he said, a twinkle in his eye as he reached out to slip his arm around her waist. "Come here, darlin'," he drawled.

She wriggled away. "All right. I like your kisses. Just no more bets."

"Scared you'll lose again?" he asked with amusement in his eyes as he teased her. "Or are you scared because you might discover that I can change more easily than you can?"

Exasperated, she turned to him. "Oh, you would so lose that bet. I work for someone else, so I have to adapt constantly to something new. You run your own business and you, Sam Gordon, are accustomed to getting your way in life. Most of the time," she added with emphasis. One corner of his mouth lifted in a crooked grin that added to her impatience with him. "Smile all you want—there is no way on earth that you are more adaptable than I am. Something impossible to prove, so you will probably argue about it on into the sunset."

"You're getting all worked up over the wrong things. Lila, stop fighting me. Things are exciting, sexy and can be so fine between us. Go with it and see what happens. We might have something really good together if you'll give us a chance."

They stood in silence and their clash of wills was palpable.

"Come on. We'll look for a room for a nursery," Sam said. "That's what we started out to do."

She nodded and walked with him. When they reached the second-floor hall, memories came of the night she had spent with him. He stopped and turned her to face him, looking directly into her eyes.

"You're remembering our night together." Sam wound his fingers in her hair. "That night was unforgettable. It was special to me before I found out that you're pregnant from our time together. Darlin', I've never had a night like that one," he said quietly. "I remember every moment and I'm guessing you do, too. Admit you remember," he coaxed in a husky tone that strummed over her raw nerves.

His fingers in her hair made her scalp tingle. He stood too close again and his gaze immobilized her. She couldn't get her breath because all she could think about was their lovemaking. Hopelessly ensnared, she looked at his mouth. As he drew her to him, he wrapped her in his embrace.

Running her hands along his strong arms, she stood on tiptoe while he kissed her. Her heart pounded and she ached with wanting him. The few kisses they'd had already had fanned flames of desire to a raging fire. She wanted Sam, wanted his loving, wanted his fun, wanted his tenderness, in spite of knowing it was an impossible situation.

She poured her passion into her kiss, hoping if she could become satiated, she would cool and her responses to him would settle. No one person had ever stirred her the way Sam could. Of all the men on earth, why Sam? Why someone from Royal with old-fashioned beliefs? But he was a sexy man filled with excitement and more perception than she had given him credit for, because he had figured out her pregnancy.

"See, you respond to me, just as I do you," Sam said after releasing her abruptly. He combed his fingers though her hair. "You set me on fire, Lila. If you'll give us a chance, there could be all sorts of good things in our lives. The loving is fantastic between us. In truth, you can't deny it."

"It's lust, Sam. Maybe I can't deny that we're

attracted, but that doesn't change some basic aspirations and principles we each have."

"A relationship between us can be more than lust. And a relationship changes everything," he argued.

He released her slightly, both breathing deeply while he gazed at her. "We can have a terrific life together," he stated. "All I want is a chance while you're here in town. Go out with me tomorrow night. Let me take you to dinner at Claire's or out of Royal. You can give me that much of a chance for us to be together. Let's see if we can't get closer to working things out between us. Will you go to dinner with me?"

"Sam—"

"Look, we need to celebrate. A baby is wonderful. Let's set the future, all these worries, aside and just celebrate the little person who will come into our world."

Suddenly, she wanted to step into his arms, hold him and have him hold her. She wanted this baby to be loved and come into a family with love. Sam's words about celebration made a knot in her throat and she was torn more than ever, discovering facets to him tonight she would have never guessed he had.

"Don't make me fall in love with you," she whispered.

"Why would that be so bad?"

"We're not alike and we'll never be able to get along."

"That's not so, Lila. We can get to know each other, darlin'. In the meantime we have tomorrow night. Let's celebrate our baby."

His words twisted her heart. She nodded, feeling the threat of tears. He made her want the celebration for the reasons he had stated and he made her want to be a couple to bring this baby into a loving family.

"Yes," she replied. Either way she answered, she would have regrets. He had just given her positive reasons to want to be with him. A celebration—never in her wildest wishes had she even considered the possibility of Sam reacting to her news in the manner he was. She wanted to be with him. At the same time, she was positive if she encouraged him, he would step into her life and take charge.

He pulled her into his arms to kiss her and, temporarily, she let go of worries about the differences. He leaned down to kiss her briefly and then just held her.

"You are fighting yourself," he whispered. "I can see it, Lila. We have a baby between us now. You can't shove that situation aside and go your damned independent way. Love between a man and woman, I think, is a foundation for a family filled with love. We have something wonderful looming in our lives if you'll just recognize and cherish it," he said.

Her heart thudded. Torn between longing for the paradise she'd had with him that one night and the realities of life with all of Sam's beliefs, she shook her head even though she wanted to hug him and forget everything else.

"Sam, let's look at this house of yours," she whispered, turning to walk away, heading blindly down the hall when she didn't know where she was going.

Catching up with her, he draped his arm across her shoulders to walk close beside her. "All right, we'll look at rooms."

His arguments tugged at her emotions. His comments carried more power to move her than she had ever expected. Sam was already formidable to deal with.

She noticed that the upstairs hall was a repeat of the downstairs in the basic decor—tall palms, framed traditional Western art on the walls. Silk-covered settees, benches, interspersed with more plants of different varieties. His house was a sales pitch for his construction business. It was beautifully furnished and he had already told her the names of the interior-decorating firms that had worked with him.

They reached the end of the hall and as he started to go through a door, she paused. "Sam, this is your room. I've seen it and you're not renovating your suite to build the nursery in with you, so there's no point in us being here."

"I thought you might want to start there and see my room again. We have memories there."

"Nice try, but no thanks. Now, where from here would you want a nursery?"

"Darlin', you're just way too much all business. Let's look at the suite closest to mine."

He led her to another suite of rooms furnished in antique George II furniture with deep blue upholstery, a thick oriental rug centered in the room on a polished oak floor.

"This is a beautiful room that's close to you."

"Close is good," he said.

"I really think you'll have to make these decisions yourself. You know how close you want a nursery."

"I want you to be happy about it and approve of it. If you lived here, where would you put the nursery and playroom?"

"You do surprise me," she admitted.

"See, there are depths to me you didn't know about," he said lightly, but his voice and his expression were serious.

"I'd say this is the perfect room."

"Then this will be the nursery." He linked her arm in his. "Let's go get some dinner and talk about some harmless, less volatile subjects and just relax a little. This has been a surprise for both of us and a shock to you tonight to realize that I've guessed the truth."

"Yes, it has," she admitted, walking beside him.

"Do you own a home in California?"

"No, a condo," she replied while they headed downstairs and outside, where he'd had a new outdoor kitchen installed. He was cheerful, keeping on harmless topics, making her laugh and relax around him as he broiled steaks and served dinner.

She could eat little, but she was having a good time with him while they avoided the topic she was certain he was thinking about as much as she.

"See, I have eight bedrooms in this place. We've already selected one for the nursery and it was quick and easy. We can agree on some things. Also, I wish you would get the decorator you want, make the decisions about the decor and all that. I don't know one thing about kids. You've already had practice with the children's center, although don't copy what you did at the club, because I don't want to feel like I'm at the club when I'm home."

"All right, I'll look into it, Sam," she said, making a commitment that would throw them together. She suspected Sam would have all sorts of requests to come that would keep them together. "We have time to plan."

He changed the subject and talked about events in Royal, harmless topics that made her laugh. Even so, she couldn't stop thinking about the baby, her pregnancy, their future and the different man she had seen in Sam earlier tonight.

It was past eleven when she stood. "Sam, I should go home now. I do get tired. It's been a fun evening, but we're both avoiding talking about the baby. I assume you plan to talk about it tomorrow night."

"I'd like to. I've made arrangements about a nursery, verified that you're pregnant. That's progress. We'll take this a bit at a time. If you have anything you feel is urgent to discuss, don't hesitate."

"I won't," she said, feeling only a degree of relief that he wasn't causing a huge problem about her pregnancy, because she was certain the issues were yet to come.

Still keeping the conversation light, flirting with her, he drove her to the Double H. As they went up the walk to the porch, he glanced at the house.

"There are lights on—are your folks waiting up?"

"Heavens, no. They both probably went to sleep an hour or so ago. They just leave lights on for me. Maybe for Hack, although heaven knows where he is. He's probably staying with a friend in Royal."

At the door, Sam turned to place his hands on her waist. "Lila, I'm thrilled beyond anything I can say."

"You astound me with your reaction when this is an unplanned baby."

"As far as I'm concerned, babies are a gift. I think it's wonderful and tomorrow night will be purely a celebration. We can shove the worries and disputes to a later date."

"I can't argue that one," she said. "Actually, I'm stunned."

"If so, maybe there's more to me than you thought. I imagine there's a lot we can discover about each other. And some things we already know are fabulous," he drawled, looking at her mouth.

She drew a deep breath and then closed her eyes as he leaned closer to kiss her, a tender kiss that lasted seconds and then transformed, becoming passionate, steamy and stirring desire.

He set her on fire with longing to make love. She clung to him, still divided emotionally by desire, shock over his responses and the wisdom to know that she couldn't live with him or accept a long-term commitment.

When she stepped away, she gasped for breath. "Thanks for taking the news in the manner you did, because it made tonight much easier for me. Thanks, too, for dinner."

He smiled and caressed her cheek. "Ah, Lila, you can't imagine how I want you. I'm glad tonight was easier for you. When we go out tomorrow, I hope to have an awesome celebration."

She smiled. "I'm still in shock over that. I don't know how I'll get one hour of sleep tonight."

"I can definitely do something about that," he drawled, lowering his voice and making her toes curl. "Come back home with me and I promise you hours of sleep—maybe a few hours from now."

She laughed and shook her head. "You're temptation, Sam Gordon. Go home. I'll see you, all too soon."

"Won't be all too soon for me, Lila. I can't wait."

"Good night, Sam." She went inside and looked out the window to see him standing by the driver's side of his car. He waved to her and she smiled again as she returned the wave.

The following day, Lila spent the morning talking to one of the men whose ranch she planned on using in the movie. It was after one o'clock when she returned to the Double H and she was tired, wanting a nap, something she had not needed in the afternoon since too far back to remember.

When she got home, everyone was away except Agnes, the cook who had worked for them since Lila was three years old. Lila sat in the kitchen eating some of Agnes's chicken salad and sliced tomatoes, talking while the older woman snapped green beans.

The doorbell chimed and Agnes dried her hands, telling Lila she would get the door. Agnes smoothed gray hair away from her face as she left the kitchen, while Lila continued eating, hearing

Agnes talking to someone but giving little thought to who it could be until the cook reappeared, hidden behind a huge bouquet of mixed flowers of all various shades of blue and pink. Lila hurried to help take the giant bouquet in its beautiful crystal vase, but Agnes set it down quickly.

"For you, Miss Lila," Agnes said, smiling broadly, her blue eyes twinkling as her gaze roamed over Lila.

"Agnes, you know I'm pregnant, don't you?" Lila asked.

"I thought so." They looked at each other another moment and then Lila hugged Agnes. "Mom knows, but Dad and Hack don't."

Agnes chuckled. "I know."

"Was it that obvious?" Lila asked.

"I wondered. You've had some morning sickness and you're beginning to show just a little."

"If you're observant," Lila remarked. "Not like Dad and Hack, which is just as well. Although I'll announce it before I go back to California."

"Your mom is happy and worried. I can tell that, too." Agnes turned toward the bouquet. "They are lovely flowers. My goodness. Aren't they pretty?"

"Yes, they are," Lila said, looking at a miniature teddy bear and a dainty, tiny doll tied in the center of a beautiful big bow of pink and blue ribbon.

She had to smile as she picked up the card and withdrew it. "I am so excited. Love, Sam."

She looked at the word *love* and shook her head. He had used the endearment as casually as calling her *sugar* and with the same depth of meaning, yet the flowers were gorgeous and the card was sweet, the whole thought very nice. Never once had she anticipated the enthusiasm that he expressed over her unplanned pregnancy. She was also thankful her dad wasn't home. She would get rid of the doll and the tiny bear, which, with blue and pink flowers, would give away that a baby was expected.

In spite of her feelings about Sam's chauvinistic views, she was as pleased by his flowers as she had been by his dinner invitation.

"Those are beautiful. So very nice," Agnes said, still admiring her flowers. "Someone is happy with you and wants to impress you."

"They're very pretty and it's sweet of him. They're from Sam Gordon."

"Ah, Mr. Gordon is a nice man. He's a very sweet man," Agnes said, her voice full of approval. "One of the best guests your dad has. And a good friend of the family."

"He is that, all right," she said, thinking about how much like her dad Sam had always seemed.

"Your brother or your dad can put the flowers where you want them. That is a heavy bouquet."

"I can lift it," Lila said, amused and sure it wouldn't harm her to carry a bouquet of flowers from one room to another. "I'll wait and see where Mom would most like to have them."

"You don't carry those flowers. You want them moved, please tell me," Agnes said firmly, giving Lila such a look that Lila nodded.

"Yes, I'll tell you, Agnes. Thank you."

Smiling, Agnes returned to snapping beans while Lila continued to admire her bouquet.

In the late afternoon she showered to get ready for her dinner date. After drying her hair, she dressed in a sleeveless fitted black cotton dress that had a straight skirt. Although her waist had thickened, she was relieved to get out of the tops that covered it and to shed the sweaters she had been wearing. As she had the night before, her mother appeared before it was time for Sam.

"Lila, I saw your gorgeous bouquet and the lovely crystal vase from Sam. That was incredibly sweet of him to send those flowers. That's a magnificent bouquet and vase."

"It's sort of overwhelming, but you're right—it is thoughtful."

"The flowers are pink and blue. I'm also glad you decided to tell him."

"I didn't tell him. He guessed."

"Then Sam is an observant man. That's one place you misjudged him. Your father still doesn't have any idea about you."

"Mom, I can't deal with Dad, too, right now. I can't have both of them pressuring me to marry."

"There's no need to say anything to the rest of the family yet. You and Sam come to some decisions first."

"We're going out tonight to celebrate the news."

"That's wonderful. I hope you appreciate it and I hope you both have a wonderful evening."

"Sam has surprised me, but don't get your hopes

up that we'll get together. Sam is like a protégé of Dad's. He has the same old-fashioned view of women and the world and I can't live with that. I know you have and you've been happy, but I'm different."

"Maybe so. The main thing is, just give Sam a chance. You keep an open mind. Remember, you're responsible not just for you but for your baby, too. I think it's wonderful that Sam wants to take you out to celebrate tonight."

"I'll admit, I'm happy about that, too. I'm really pleased he feels that way. When confronted with an unexpected pregnancy, not all bachelors would want to celebrate. Sam hasn't proposed, but I expect him to do so. It would go against all his beliefs to not propose," Lila said as she brushed her hair.

"Just be tolerant and think over a proposal before you turn him down."

"All right," she said, smiling, knowing she would do what she wanted and there was no way she would marry Sam and settle in Royal.

"I'll go wait," Barbara said, glancing at herself in the mirror. "I enjoy talking to him. How

I wish your brother would pay attention and try to emulate Sam." Barbara sighed and got up to leave the room.

"Thanks, Mom," Lila said, grateful for her mother and the close bond they shared. She turned to her mirror to study her image. She had her hair up on her head in a fancy sterling clip.

Her black dress was longer than usual, the hem midcalf, but with a slit on one side that revealed her leg up to midthigh when she walked.

She didn't hear the chimes, but her mother informed her of Sam's approach. With one last look in the mirror, Lila left to greet Sam.

Seven

When Lila walked into the living room, both Sam and her dad stood until she was seated. Smiling at her, Sam's gaze swept over her. Nearby on the back of the grand piano was the bouquet of flowers, looking as gorgeous as ever.

"Hi, Sam," she said, smiling at him with her heartbeat pounding faster. "My flowers are beautiful. Thank you."

"I'm glad you like them," he replied.

"Flowers are nice," Beau said. "In August in the West Texas heat, it takes an ocean of water to keep any flowers alive. Is there an occasion for these flowers?"

"Yes," Sam replied, and Lila held her breath. "I asked Lila to dinner tonight and she accepted so I thought flowers might be nice for the fancy Hollywood lady."

She smiled at him in relief. "They're very nice wherever I'm from."

"You're a Texan, honey, now and forever," Beau said. "I've been thinking about calling you, Sam. I thought I'd run into you at the club, but then each time I forgot to talk to you. I want to build another house for a new hand. I want you to do the building."

"Sure. We can talk about it anytime. I'll call you tomorrow," Sam said.

Lila listened to their conversation, participating when they changed the topic, thinking how formal and polite they were, yet the sight of Sam in a charcoal suit with a snowy shirt, his navy tie, set her pulse racing. In spite of her worries, anticipation was paramount. A celebration with Sam was too appealing for her to be filled with dread over arguments to come.

When they were in his car, he turned to her. "I have an airplane waiting. How's Dallas? I considered Claire's but thought you might prefer Dallas since maybe you'd rather keep talk down in Royal about us being a couple."

"Frankly, I would," she said, thinking about Royal's elegant restaurant but preferring the anonymity of Dallas.

"Whatever you want, darlin'," he replied. Sam drove them to the small airport where a pilot waited with Sam's private plane.

Once at the restaurant in Dallas, she sat across from Sam at a table covered in white linen. He leaned back and unfastened his coat to let it swing open. Sam always oozed self-confidence, which probably was part of his take-charge personality.

He took her hand and smiled at her. Once again, for a moment a pang rocked her while she wished life was different and Sam held fresh, contemporary views.

"What would you like to drink?"

"Ginger ale is my preference."

He smiled, candlelight highlighting his cheekbones, giving a warm tint to his tan skin. "I'll have that with you, then."

Smiling, she shook her head. "You don't need to drink ginger ale."

Before he could answer, their waiter appeared and Sam ordered two ginger ales.

"That's ridiculous. Get a glass of wine, beer, whatever you like."

"When you can drink wine, I'll drink wine. Right now, you do what is healthy and I'll join you."

Looking at the dimly lit restaurant that held a small dance floor, a fountain at one end of the room, tables centered with candles in hurricane lamps, she thought of the unbridgeable chasm between them—one that she couldn't change any more than Sam could change how he felt. There was no future for them. She had to get along with Sam since he would be in her life for many years because of one strong tie. But she didn't expect to share many nights like tonight. She looked into his eyes, and it was as if a fist squeezed her heart.

He was handsome: thickly lashed blue eyes, symmetrical features, his straight, neat brown hair, a firm jaw, his straight nose. The charcoal suit gave him a commanding appearance. White cuffs showed at his wrists with gold cufflinks catching light from the candle's flame. If only he didn't hold such outdated views of women.

He gazed back, holding her hand, his thumb running slowly back and forth over her knuckles so lightly, yet she felt his touch to her toes.

"Thank you again for the beautiful flowers."

"They're a token—hopefully, something that represents joy and wonderful expectations. Lila, I'm excited. A baby seems a miracle."

She tilted her head to study him. "You amaze me. I would never have guessed your reaction to the news that you'll be a dad. You seem opposed to children at the club and yet you turn right around and seem dazzled over the prospect of having your own baby. That's an enormous contradiction that I didn't expect."

"It's how I feel on both subjects. I am dazzled over the prospect because my own baby is a miracle. Every baby is, and that has nothing to do with kids in the TCC children's center. Our baby, Lila. That just staggers me. I'm restraining myself—I want to whoop and holler and I can't stop grinning when I think about it. I can't whoop and holler here, and we'll have to toast the event with ginger ale, but I'm so excited I'm babbling."

He grinned broadly, a happy smile that made her heart thud, and she couldn't resist smiling at him in return. Startling her, he moved the candle out of the way, leaned across the table to draw her closer and kissed her hard. After the first startled second, she returned his kiss. She was oblivious to their surroundings as she kissed him. Joy tinged with a sadness filled her.

Finally, he sat back in his chair. "I'm thrilled beyond words."

"I'm glad but still shocked. Your past never gave a hint that you would react this way. You voted against women joining the Texas Cattleman's Club, and against the child-care center. If you could vote again tomorrow, you'd still vote that way, wouldn't you?"

"I think so. I don't expect our baby to be in a child-care center. Before, I never thought about the children's center in terms of myself. I've told you why I voted like I did. The club was started as a male haven. I don't see why the ladies don't have their own club. And they do have some clubs in Royal and men aren't trying to crash them. Actually, that's insignificant and tonight I'd like to stay off the subject because I want this night to be a celebration of our baby. That's the most important thing in my life right now."

"I can't argue with you on that one."

He glanced toward the dance floor. "There are some couples dancing. Let's join them."

He stood, still holding her hand, and she rose to go with him. As soon as they were on the dance floor, he wrapped her into his arms to dance. She was close against him, moving slowly with him. As always, the dance became sensual, stirring desire. The piano player sang the romantic lyrics that she knew by memory. This night with Sam would remain a memory forever.

Beautiful flowers, this dinner, his attitude about the baby, no proposal, a joyful celebration tonight—he amazed her in all those things.

They danced slowly and returned to their table when the song ended. As he held her chair and seated her, he caressed her nape, a feathery brush of his fingers that made her tingle.

Their drinks had been served, and Sam picked

up his glass of the bubbly clear liquid. "Here's to our baby, Lila, and to you, my baby's mother."

"Thank you, Sam." Smiling at him, she lifted her glass. She raised it to touch his lightly before taking a sip of the ginger ale.

She raised her glass again. "Here's to you, Sam, for your understanding, for not rushing into an instant plan, especially for not proposing the minute you heard the news."

"A proposal would be so terrible, Lila?" He waved his hand. "Don't even answer. I told you that tonight is a celebration—one of the happiest occasions of my life. I don't want any controversy, even in fun. Let's stay off the thin-ice topics tonight."

"Once again, I won't argue with you. This is a wonderful evening, Sam."

He gave her such a warm look she wondered whether he had mistaken that as an invitation to seduction. "Great," he said, lifting his glass to her. They both took another drink and set down their glasses.

He took her hand, holding it gently and running his thumb over the back of her hand and her wrist, light brushes that she should have been able to ignore but couldn't. He was doing everything right and it was beginning to unnerve her.

"Have you made any plans regarding our baby?" Sam asked.

"Not really. I've just been getting accustomed to the idea. I've let them know at work and I'll take time off. My mom knows. I told Shannon and of course, my California doctor knows."

"You don't have a doctor in Royal?"

"I have my family doctor, but not anyone I've seen about this."

"I think you should see a doctor here or in Midland—I'll take you to Midland if you prefer. You never know when you might need one, and for the sake of the baby, I think you should have a record established with a doctor you want. If there's an emergency, you don't want to meet a new doctor for the first time."

"I suppose you make sense and I should," she said.

"I'd feel better about it, both for your sake and the baby's."

She nodded. "All right, Sam. You win this one."

"I'm not trying to fight with you, Lila. I really want what's best for you and our baby."

"I have to admit, you surprise me more and more. You're not doing anything the way I expected. You have won the Most Unpredictable Man title over this."

He smiled in return and raised his glass of ginger ale in a toast. She touched her glass to his and sipped, laughing as she set it down.

"Have you thought of any names?"

"I'm debating about later and whether or not I want to know if I'll have a boy or a girl. At this point, no, I'm not thinking about names. It's too early."

"Do I get input?"

"Yes. I don't promise to let you name our baby, but I'm willing to listen."

"Good. When you decide to go public, let me know. I'd like to tell Josh. With our dad gone, we're basically all the family we have. There are cousins and aunts and uncles, but no one who lives out this way and none we're close to."

"I will soon, but not quite yet. I have to make some decisions first and I really would rather everyone in Royal know about the baby after I've gone back to California."

"Whatever you want," he said. "You said your mom knows—how does she feel about it? This will be her first grandchild."

"I think she's excited and she's supportive, but this is new to her. I'm guessing her real excitement will come when she holds her grandbaby in her arms."

"I imagine you're right, there."

"She likes you very much, so you have an advocate."

"Do I need an advocate?"

"Not really, at this point. She also thinks the flowers are beautiful."

"Flowers, taking you to dinner—those are things that I can do. What I feel like doing is dancing down Main Street and through the TCC, shouting to everyone I see that I am going to become a dad. Don't worry, I won't really do it yet. I might not be able to control myself when this baby comes into the world. We have a miracle, Lila."

"You sound convincing, as if you really mean that."

"I mean it with my whole heart," he said, his sincere tone and blue-eyed gaze giving emphasis to his words. "This is the most fabulous thing in my life."

"I'm repeating myself, but I never, ever for one second expected you to react the way you have."

"See, you don't know me all that well. But you will," he added softly, his voice holding sensual promises. "In truth, I've been a little astounded myself at how I feel. I've never given little kids a thought, because I'm never around them. We didn't have younger siblings. They just haven't been part of my life and I never would have guessed I'd feel this way, but this is my baby, Lila. I'm thrilled."

Growing solemn, she studied him. He might turn out to be far more of a problem than she had dreamed if he was locked into wanting his baby in his life. This was not something she had factored in when she had thought about Sam's reaction to the news. He had been so opposed to the child-care center that she had never imagined he would be thrilled to become a dad. And he was becoming far more appealing to her—something that could prove her undoing.

The waiter arrived to take their orders and she withdrew her hand from Sam's. As she ordered the grilled salmon, Sam waited, looking mildly amused, and she was certain it was because she had insisted on ordering for herself. He probably had ordered for every other woman he had ever taken out from the moment he had started dating.

Next, she listened while he ordered a prime rib.

"Thank you for letting me place my order," she said as soon as they were alone.

"There's no way I want to infringe on your independence in stuff like ordering dinner. That's not one of life's real issues."

"It is rather well known that leopards don't change their spots, so that was a leap for you."

"I can adapt and I can definitely try to please you," he said in a huskier voice. "That's what I most like to do." He took her hand again. "I would like to spend hours tonight, darlin', just trying to pleasure you," he said softly. His tone conveyed far more than his words and she tingled when she heard his thick, husky drawl.

"Sam, maybe I've underestimated you. You want to spend hours together tonight—that just makes my heart race," she replied in her own sultry tone, unable to resist flirting with him and letting go of worries for a while.

His blue eyes darkened and he inhaled deeply, taking her hand and placing a light kiss on her palm. He held her hand, resting his on the table. "Now, that, Lila, makes me want to chuck dinner and head for a private place where I can 'pleasure' you for hours."

"But we'll do what's sensible and sit and talk about our future," she said with great innocence, still having fun flirting with him. "But I do feel better, Sam, that you're being positive," she stated.

"A simple compliment that I will definitely reply to before this evening is over," he said softly, his voice becoming velvet, having the same effect as a caress.

"I think it's time we change the subject."

"For now, maybe, but we'll continue the conversation later back at my place."

"Back at your place? Sam, your self-confidence

overwhelms me. Brace yourself—back at your place might not happen tonight."

"If it doesn't, it doesn't. We'll see," he said with all the certainty in his statement that he would have had if she had flatly accepted. His confident smile indicated what he expected to do when they returned to Royal.

"So you worked in your office today or in Pine Valley where you're building?" she asked, knowing she should stop flirting and keep space between them because she did not want a seduction scene later in the night.

"I have four houses right now that are under construction, and I spent time at one first and then another. Two are in Pine Valley. I was at my office and at the club. At the club, all the men can talk about is Alex Santiago's disappearance. As far as I know, there's still no word on Alex."

"The few times I've seen Nathan, he looks preoccupied, as if he's worried," Lila said, withdrawing her hand from Sam's.

"The last two times I've been at the club, rumors have been going around that Chance may have had something to do with Alex's disappearance."

"Why would Chance do anything to harm Alex?"

"A woman is why," Sam replied. "Cara Windsor. Chance dated her and then she fell in love with Alex."

"Chance doesn't seem like the type to harm someone, but I don't know him that well."

"I agree with you. I know one thing—the last conversation I had with Alex, which was shortly before his disappearance, was interrupted by Dave Firestone, who was mad as hell. I left, so I didn't hear what the heated exchange was about, but they were angry with each other."

"That doesn't sound so good. Have you told Nathan?"

"No, but I'm thinking maybe I should, with all the rumors flying about Chance."

"I'd think so. It might be important. It would be terrible for them to focus on the wrong person," she said, thinking more about Sam than the rumors.

Salads appeared and they paused in the conversation until the waiter had gone.

While they ate, Sam kept her entertained. She

ate lightly, declining a dessert. Sam was showing his best side, handsome, charming, doing all the right things.

They danced until ten and then flew back to Royal. "Come by my house, Lila. It's not too late and we can sit and talk."

"Sam—"

"We'll talk. I'll take you home whenever you want. C'mon. Better sitting with me than going home and sitting up with Hack."

"My brother," she said, shaking her head and smiling. "This summer, you'll always win with that argument. Okay, briefly."

The moment she agreed, Sam changed course to drive them to his home in Pine Valley.

When they reached his house, Sam directed her to the kitchen. "We'll get something to drink while we talk. You're limited in your drinks. Want another ginger ale, milk, hot chocolate? I have a veritable grocery store here. What would you like?"

"Actually, hot chocolate sounds the best," she said.

"Lila, this is good tonight because I want us to

get to know each other. I know a lot about your family from being friends with your folks, although I see far less of your mother than your dad."

While he talked, he removed his charcoal jacket and tie, rolled up his sleeves. He unbuttoned the top buttons of his shirt. When he reached the third button, he glanced at her to catch her watching him. Blushing, she turned away, wishing she had done something besides stare at him as he made himself comfortable.

"You can unbutton all you want, too," he said.

His words ended her embarrassment and tension. She smiled at him. "Thanks for the offer," she remarked dryly. "I think I'll keep it together."

He walked over to her. "I know one thing that can go and I hope you don't object." He removed the sterling clip holding her hair. Auburn locks tumbled to her shoulders. He placed the clip on a small table and then combed his fingers through her hair while they gazed into each other's eyes. "You know this is the way I like your hair—down, falling free. Your hair is gorgeous, Lila."

"Thank you," she whispered, looking at his

mouth while he stood so close. Her breath caught as she looked into his eyes.

She expected him to kiss her, anticipated his kiss and then was surprised when he turned away. "Hot chocolate it is," he said.

She tried to ignore the flash of disappointment. He was doing what she wanted, so she should be relieved they hadn't kissed.

As soon as he had their drinks, they strolled to the adjoining living area that overlooked the patio and sparkling blue pool. She sat in a corner of a sofa and he sat beside her, closer than she had expected. There was a table beside her and one in front of the sofa, so they had places to set their drinks.

"Tonight has been fun. I'm excited, Lila. This is my first child. How could I possibly keep from being excited?"

She had to laugh at him. "You have six months to go. Some of that excitement may wear off."

"I think it may grow instead of diminishing."

"If it grows much more, I think you really will be dancing around town." She smiled at him. "I've had fun tonight, Sam. It's been enjoyable, surprising, but the problems will come."

"We can weather them," he said.

"Your supreme self-confidence is always with you."

"How much do you know about babies, Lila?"

"Nothing. I was around Hack, but I was a kid myself, albeit a bigger kid than Hack. I'm reading about parenting and I'll take a class."

"Oh, yes. I should take a class in being a dad and we probably should go together to a class on childbirth."

"I'll be in California, remember?"

"You'll come back to Texas to have your baby, won't you? I'd think your mom would want you to."

"She's already talking and making plans as if I'd agreed to do so, but I haven't."

"It would be really nice to have a Texas birthplace."

She laughed. "You get a gold star tonight for tact," she said, unable to keep from noticing the open throat of his shirt, which revealed his chest and the thick mat of curly light brown chest hair that Lila knew from memory.

"Whatever you decide. I know I don't have any influence on that one." He set down his drink and crossed the room to pick up his coat and rummage in the pocket. He held out a package wrapped in shiny blue paper and tied with a big pink silk bow. "For you, darlin'."

Surprised, she glanced at the small package and then looked at him.

"Go ahead, Lila. It's a present for you."

"Sam, you don't need to get me presents and flowers."

"I don't need to. I want to," he said as she opened the box. He sat down again beside her.

She placed the paper and bow on the coffee table and opened the box to see a gold heart-shaped necklace covered in diamonds.

"This is gorgeous," she said.

"Open it."

"It opens? It's a locket?" She pulled it open and a tiny folded paper fell out. She picked it up to unfold it and read tiny print: "For our baby's picture. Sam."

"Sam, that is so sweet. I'm touched by this and I'll treasure it." When she snapped the locket shut, she turned it over. The smooth back was gold with the current date inscribed. "You have today's date," she said, glancing at him.

"That's to remember the night we celebrated our little one's arrival."

Impulsively, she threw her arms around his neck to kiss him lightly. "Thank you. It's beautiful and that is just so sweet of you. Put it on me, Sam."

He took it from her and set it in the box on the table. "I will put it on you, but not right this minute. Come here, darlin'," he said, lifting her to his lap. "Ah, Lila, I've been wanting to bring you home with me and do this since you walked into the front room at the Double H hours ago."

Her heartbeat raced while she looked up at him. His mouth was only inches away and the look in his blue eyes conveyed his intentions. As longing pulsed with each heartbeat, she wrapped her arms around his neck.

"I'm already caught in a tangled situation that I can't control. May as well be hanged for a sheep as a goat, as the old saying goes," she whispered.

His attention was on her mouth and she raised her lips to his. His kiss was possessive, seductive, fanning the flames of desire that already consumed her. She loved being in his arms, being held by him, kissed by him, returning his kisses.

How was she going to say no to him and keep him at arm's length? At the moment, she didn't want to, which was what had placed her in this situation. Why did they have this magic chemistry between them that she had never found with any other man?

Running her fingers in his hair, she moaned softly, longing for so much more from him, wanting another night of loving. She pressed more tightly against him, kissing him with the same passion with which he kissed her.

She barely felt his fingers moving on her, but soon cool air brushed her shoulders and the top of her dress fell to her waist. Sam leaned back to gaze at her with half-lidded eyes while he removed her lacy black bra. As he caressed her, she shifted up her skirt to sit astride him.

Placing her hands on either side of his face, she leaned forward to kiss him, pouring her desire, her feelings for him, into her kiss. Every move was a mistake, but at this point she didn't care. She had had a wonderful time with him. He had hidden all the take-charge, chauvinistic, arrogant ways he had. Not once in the evening had he demonstrated any of them in a manner that had annoyed her. She hadn't seen them at all. And without those ways, he was delightful, appealing, incredibly sexy.

"Sam, you don't fight fair. You can be the most irresistible man."

"I don't want to fight you at all," he whispered while his tongue followed the curve of her ear, sending tingles in its wake.

He leaned back to look at her, cupping her breasts in his hands. "You're the most beautiful woman on earth, Lila. Each time I see you, you dazzle me and I want you in my arms," he whispered before leaning forward to trail kisses over her soft breasts.

His words enticed her as much as his kisses. She couldn't possibly believe him, but his declarations still carried a thrill of pleasure.

"This has already been lonely and difficult in

some ways, Sam," she whispered. "I want your kisses tonight, your arms around me, your reassurances," she admitted, knowing there would be some really tough decisions and moments ahead.

"You don't have to be lonely and have a difficult time," he whispered between showering kisses over her. He raised his head to look into her eyes. "Lila, that's your own doing and your own choice. I will do anything for you, darlin'," he promised softly. "I'll guarantee you won't be lonely and you won't be alone having our baby."

The thrill of his promise was as devastating as his kisses. His mouth was firm on hers. Kissing her passionately, he made her ache for him and moan in pleasure.

Tugging his shirt out of his slacks, her fingers twisted free his buttons until she could push his shirt off his shoulders to toss it away. Running her hands over his chest, feeling as if she couldn't get enough of him this night, she kissed along his throat, moving down while he caressed her breasts.

Her need built, burning like flames licking over her. She stepped off him, standing beside the sofa to pull him to his feet. He stood, towering over her even though she was tall. Her heart pounded with fiery longing and another shock: that he was causing her to fall in love with him.

When he swept her into his arms to kiss her, she locked her arms around his neck. Carrying her through the room into the hall to a downstairs bedroom, he set her on her feet and held her away from him to push her dress over her hips and let it fall in a soft pile around her ankles. "Lila, you take my breath," he whispered. "You're beautiful, darlin'."

Lila kicked off her shoes while he continued to look at her in a long, slow perusal that made her quiver and sent her temperature soaring.

"Sam," she whispered, fumbling with his belt to unbuckle it and pull it off. Wanting him with all her being, she unfastened his slacks, pushing away his briefs to free him.

She stood gazing at him as thoroughly as he studied her and then she knelt to stroke and kiss him.

Threading his fingers in her hair, he groaned. Her fingers drifted down his muscled legs, feeling the crisp, short hairs. Suddenly he slipped his hands beneath her arms to pull her up, wrapping her in a tight embrace while he kissed her hard, his tongue going deep.

Her heart raced. Heat pooled low inside her, a yearning for him that filled her. Tomorrow ceased to exist and yesterday had already passed. There was only the present with his kisses and caresses and endearments. For now, that was what she craved and wanted to give to him in turn. Another night of love between them that might mean something in her memories when this was no longer possible.

He picked her up to place her on the bed and began to shower kisses lightly below her ear, along her throat, moving down over her, caressing her, as if every inch of her was important to him, whispering endearments between his kisses.

"Darlin', you're gorgeous. Ah, baby, you're perfection, the most beautiful woman ever. Love, you can't ever know what you do to me."

His whispered words could make her feel as if she were the most desirable woman on earth, and how could she resist that? She knew he could not mean all of them, exaggerations in the throes of passion, but she liked having his hands and mouth on her, his words reflecting his desire.

"Sam, let's make love. Come here," she whispered, pulling him to her.

He moved between her legs, pausing to look at her. It gave her a chance to view him. He looked strong, virile, handsome. She caressed his muscled thighs and then tugged lightly on him.

"Come here," she whispered.

As he lowered himself, he held his weight off her slightly while he entered her with deliberate slowness.

Gasping with need, she arched beneath him and wrapped her arms around him.

"Put your legs around me, darlin'," he whispered.

She did as he wanted, holding him tightly, moving beneath him while he teased and increased the sweet torment until she was thrashing with need. "Love me," she pleaded.

Finally, he thrust deeply and moved, rocking with her as desire built swiftly. He pumped faster and she cried out with pleasure.

"My darling," she whispered, clinging tightly to him.

"Ah, love," he ground out the words as they soared together and then she crashed.

"Lila, my love," he gasped, thrusting deeply, shuddering with effort as he climaxed and finally lowered his weight and slowed. He gasped for breath as much as she. Blissfully, she ran her hands over him.

"Sam, that was perfect. Better than before. Everything was so wonderful tonight."

"I want to make love all night. If I could do what I want, really, we would stay in this room for the next week, maybe longer."

She scattered light kisses on his cheek and forehead until he rolled over, taking her with him. Their legs were entangled and he held her close against him as he brushed her long hair away from her face. She was damp, still breathing as hard as he.

"This is marvelous," she whispered, half hoping he didn't even hear her. She didn't need to give him more encouragement, because difficulties lay ahead and their lovemaking would not do one thing to help avoid them.

He kissed her softly, trailing his fingers over her shoulder, along her throat and then combing them through her hair. "Darlin', I want you in my arms."

"As far as I'm concerned, tonight is a time to forget the difficulties and problems."

"I'll agree with that. Tonight is fabulous. It's far from over."

"Maybe," she whispered, running her hand over his shoulder, feeling his muscles. While she snuggled against him, she ran her fingers over his shoulder again. "Where do we go from here, Sam?" she whispered, not really wanting an answer at this time. She was willing to give the night over to lovemaking and set their problems aside temporarily.

"We'll go shower after a while. Right now, let me hold you close in my arms."

"No argument here," she said, rising on her elbow to kiss his jaw and throat. "You're a handsome man and at the moment, we're a mutual-admiration twosome."

"Twosome sounds good, darlin'. Really good to me." He pulled her closer against him. "Lila, it can be so fine between us. If we'll each just give a little."

"That's a dream, but with all my heart I hope you're right," she said.

"Just try. If we both just try and aim for that as our goal, we should be able to achieve it," he whispered. "We can compromise."

"Are you going to take your own advice?"

He chuckled. "You're a hard woman some-times."

"I believe being hard belongs to you," she said, teasing him, and he smiled, kissing her forehead. She could feel his heartbeat against her. He was warm, solid muscle.

He held her close and they talked for a while before he carried her to his shower.

As she dressed, she turned to him. "Now, come put my beautiful new locket on me."

"Sure thing," he said, taking it from her and fastening it around her neck while she held her hair out of his way. He brushed light kisses on her nape and she turned to him.

"Thank you for the locket and for being so marvelous about everything."

"You're welcome, darlin'."

"Sam, I should go home."

"I guess you're right. Go out with me again. The TCC has a singer tomorrow night and the chef will have a lobster special."

"All right," she said, knowing she was sinking deeper into later complications with him. "Actually, it'll be our farewell, I imagine. I start back to work on Wednesday of next week and then I'll be too busy for anything else."

"That doesn't sound good. You're not overworked, are you?"

"I'm just busy. I'll take care of myself."

"Then we definitely go out tomorrow night. I have something special in mind."

"Now I'm curious," she said. "For now, though, I should get home."

After the drive to the ranch, she faced Sam at her doorstep. He had his hands lightly on her waist. "Lila, this has been another one-of-the-best-nights-of-my-life evening. I can't wait until tonight. It seems forever until I'll see you again."

She laughed. "Sam, you'll get through the day without me."

"Not easily. I'll pick you up at six. I have something at the house, too, I want to show you, but tonight wasn't the night. Tonight was purely celebration."

"I'm getting really curious," she said, wondering what he had planned and guessing she was in for another surprise with one of his gifts.

His arms circled her waist and he pulled her close and the kiss changed from casual to passionate.

When she stepped away, she tried to catch her breath. "I had a wonderful evening, as you know. Thank you for dinner, for my beautiful locket and thank you again for the flowers and for being so—" she paused, trying to think of something that would describe what he had done "—cooperative in your reactions."

"I don't think you really know me," he said. His expression changed as he smiled. "But you will," he said, and she had to smile in return.

"I can believe that one," she said. "Good night,

Sam." She stepped inside and in minutes heard him drive away.

Switching off the lights left on for her, she tiptoed to her room. Instead of facing Sam and getting the arguments over and done, she had gone out and had a wonderful time and accomplished nothing as far as her future was concerned. Their next dinner she would talk to him about the future and their baby. Also, he had something to give her—some delightful, touching or sweet present that would make getting serious with him more difficult.

Just hours from now, she would be with Sam. Her heart beat faster in anticipation and she shook her head. She was already a little bit in love with him. She hoped it truly was a little bit, because none of their deepest feelings and individual beliefs would change. If he continued reacting as he had so far, she would fall more in love with him. Time would tell on that. Falling in love with Sam would be disastrous because somewhere inside that handsome, sexy, charming exterior was the male chauvinist, the take-charge character she had always known, and he would come out sooner or later.

In the meantime, excitement bubbled in her over the prospect of being with him tomorrow night.

It wasn't even twenty-four hours until they would be together.

That night, she dressed in a sleeveless red dress that ended above her knees. She wore high-heeled red sandals. This would probably be the last evening she would spend with Sam, because she would be too busy once she started work. It was just as well. When her job here ended, she would return to California—maybe until after the baby was born.

Sam was in a navy cotton shirt and navy slacks, and as soon as he picked her up, they drove to his home in Pine Valley. "Let's go have one of your delicious ginger ales. I want to talk to you and I have something for you. Then we have reservations at the club—the TCC has a great singer tonight and a chef's special of lobster and steak. If that doesn't appeal to you, we can eat at my place.

I was going to do this the other way around, but I think we'll stop here first."

"Fine," she answered as she stepped out of the car, curious about the surprise. "Thank you for the gorgeous flowers that arrived today," she said, thinking of the latest bouquet, a far more traditional arrangement of mixed flowers with huge red, yellow and white roses mixed in with tall, colorful gladiolas, tiger lilies and other assorted flowers. "You've impressed my family. Even Hack didn't have any of his usual smart remarks."

"I'm glad to hear that."

"I haven't shown Dad or Hack my locket yet, because Dad will have a million questions and he'll think we're serious. I'll show him after I tell him he is going to become a grandfather."

"You know how to deal with your dad, darlin'. You and Hack both do."

"In spite of my morning sickness and seeing each other every day and living in the same house, neither Dad nor Hack has caught on that I'm pregnant."

"Hack doesn't surprise me. You're probably wallpaper to him and he doesn't even see you.

Hack's got teenage-kid things on his mind. Your dad—that's different. Sometimes we see what we want to see."

Startled, she was surprised by Sam's answer. "You might be right."

"Let's have a drink." At the bar in a family room, Sam got two ginger ales. He motioned toward the sofa and followed her to sit close, facing her. "All I've been able to think about today is you."

She had no intention of telling him she could say the same. "That will pass," she replied, smiling at him.

He raised his ginger ale. "Another toast to making memories and having a baby. Or making a baby and having memories," he said, smiling at her.

Laughing, she touched his glass with hers and sipped while watching him. He set his glass on a table and then took hers, and she wondered again what he had planned.

Taking her hand in his, he gazed at her with an earnest look on his face. "You're special, Lila, and this baby of ours is incredibly special to me."

"Sam, I'm touched."

"I was going to do this another way," he said, "take you somewhere fabulous, but at the last minute, I wanted to be just the two of us."

Puzzled, she received another shock when, still holding her hand, he knelt on one knee in front of her.

"Lila, will you marry me?"

Eight

Even though she had expected a proposal from him the moment he learned of her pregnancy, she stared in surprise. Since he had not proposed right away, she had begun to accept that he wouldn't. Her heart began to pound. "Sam, for heaven's sake." She stood to walk away from him, turning to face him when there was more space between them.

He got up and started toward her, but when she held up her hand, he stopped.

"When you didn't propose at the first opportunity, I stopped worrying about it."

"There's no reason to worry. I mean it. I want to marry you."

"I'm sure you do. I appreciate your offer very much. I have to say no. You've been wonderful, but I can't marry you."

He frowned as if it had never occurred to him that she might turn him down.

As he crossed the room to her, she locked her fingers together. She didn't want him coaxing, seducing, charming or doing anything else to win her over. He could weave a spell, but when marriage was at stake, she had no intention of succumbing.

He touched her closed fists, which were locked together. "Your hands are freezing," he declared, frowning. "Why can't you marry me?" he asked.

"We can settle this one quickly. We have vastly different philosophies of life. You don't want a wife who works outside the home. Correct?"

"No, I don't. Why would you want to if you have a baby to take care of, a mansion to tend, all the charities you want to run—"

"Stop right there," she interrupted. "It's okay for your wife to run charities, which takes hours away from home and sometimes can be as much work as a regular job, but it's not all right for your wife to be gainfully employed?"

"A charity is less stringent, less demanding and, most of the time, a hell of a lot shorter lasting and you know it, Lila," he replied. His blue eyes had darkened to the color of a stormy sky and she suspected a big storm was on her horizon with him.

"I don't know that all charities are shorter lasting. I've seen my mother work like crazy on charities. I intend to keep my job and my career. There is no way you would be happy with that, because it means I will be in California."

"I don't think you're considering our baby and I don't think you're being the least bit sensible about this."

"*Me* not being sensible?" she asked, staring at him. "That remark sounds like the Sam Gordon I know. Also, there's a far bigger reason, Sam, actually the biggest and most important reason of all—you and I are definitely not in love."

"Lila, we're wonderful together. It's been fantastic. I've told you that several times and frankly, you've said the same back to me and acted as if you were happy to be in my company. What we have between us is good enough for me and you're important enough for me to say I love you."

"Please. Don't do that now. You've never said those words to me before. Don't say them now. I have no intention of marrying without love."

Silence stretched between them. "Lila, look. I think true love will come. I feel something for you, that's certain. I want to be with you. We have a lot that's good going on between us. Other than our views of a woman's place in life, we're compatible."

"Oh, Sam, if you only stopped to listen to yourself—'a woman's place in life.' Great heavens, come into this century."

"You're so damned independent. You want to go off to California and raise our baby on your own so you can work and live as you please."

"That kind of covers it," she said, her anger growing.

"You'll struggle with being a single parent, cut our baby out of knowing, really knowing, his or her blood father, just to pursue a career. A child is forever, while a career, a job, is the most fleeting thing. Why tear up your life over a job?"

"I'm not going to argue the merits of my job with you. I want my career. Period. End of discussion."

"If you have to work, there are jobs here in Royal."

"Please. How many production-designer jobs are there?"

"Okay, so no damned movie jobs. But interesting jobs nonetheless. And you know I like being with you. I think you're messing two lives up so you can prove your so-called independence that will get you nothing. Maybe some heartaches."

She walked away from him. "We're not in love and that's the most basic reason. I don't want to marry because it will be convenient." She hurt as she turned to face him again with more distance between them. "Sam, I want love. Real love. You and I don't have that between us, and don't try to tell me you love me."

"I won't," he replied solemnly. "We could give love a chance to develop between us. Has that ever occurred to you?"

"Maybe, but if we do, we'll have to give it a chance while we're single because I won't marry in the hope that love will come."

"Are you thinking about this baby?"

"Of course I am. Do you think a child is happy with parents in a loveless marriage who married for the wrong reasons?" Hurting, she stared at Sam. He was so handsome, so appealing to her, but also so old-fashioned. She couldn't cope with that every day of her life. They were poles apart and she couldn't see how either one could change.

"I would try to make you happy, Lila," he said.

"I know you would, but it wouldn't work. You want a wife who has a certain lifestyle, who will be a wife like my mom is for my dad. You don't want to live in California and I don't want to live in Royal, because I have a career in California. We're not in love. I always come back to that because that's the big one," she said firmly, but her words seemed to ring hollow. The past few days with him had made her care more for him, but the feelings should pass because they wanted different things out of life. Each time she reminded herself there was no love between them, she had a fluttery feeling, as if she knew better than what she stated. She wasn't in love with this chauvinistic, stubborn man. She could not be in love with him.

"Sam, love can overcome all sorts of obstacles and if we were deeply in love, we would try to work things out. But we're not. You're not in love with me. You didn't even pursue seeing me after your first few calls."

"You didn't return them. I don't go where I'm not wanted."

"That's understandable, and that's all past now, anyway. You're like my dad. I am not like my mother. We don't have a future together. Face that and let's work from that point. We can work out dividing our time. Loads of couples do that."

"Doesn't make it good," he said.

"I want a marriage filled with love and someone who will support me in what I really want to do. I imagine you want that, too. Did your parents love each other?"

"As far as I know. I was so young when Mom died that I might not have noticed if they weren't happy. Actually, Dad seemed torn up when he lost her and I imagine they did love each other. I never had anything to indicate otherwise."

"Don't you want a marriage filled with love?"

"Yes, I do," he replied solemnly.

"There you are," she said with a note of finality. "Now be realistic and let's work from there. The flowers are beautiful, but stop sending them and trying to conjure up something that doesn't exist. I'll share our baby. I know this is your baby, too."

"It's going to be more difficult to work out."

"That's probably true, but marrying just to make it easy to deal with raising our baby isn't my idea of something good."

"I imagine plenty of people have married for that reason, married for the sake of a baby. I'd even guess that a lot of those marriages have worked out well and the parents have fallen in love."

"I'm not taking that chance and going into that kind of union. Or a marriage where we battle constantly over my career."

His eyes narrowed and he crossed the room to her. With a drumming heartbeat, she watched him approach. "This has to count for something," he said, wrapping his arms around her and kissing her.

At first she doubled her fists and held them back to avoid touching him. All thoughts fled and she became aware of only his kiss, what she had dreamed about, like the kisses last night, steamy kisses that melted and seduced and banished differences.

She knew what he was trying to prove—that she responded to him. Her arms circled his neck and she kissed him in return in spite of knowing her response would only encourage him to argue further.

All thought processes ceased because she was submerged in sensation. She clung to him, returning his kisses as he leaned over her and then, still kissing her, picked her up to carry her to a sofa, where he sat and cradled her against his shoulder as he kissed her.

She stopped kissing him, gazing into his eyes, feeling her heart pound because she wanted him, wanted his loving, wanted his kisses. Instead, she slipped off his lap and moved to a nearby chair to sit facing him.

"We can still spend the evening together and talk about the future and what you will do," he said quietly. "Just think about getting married. Don't say no quite so fast. That isn't asking too much, is it?"

"No, it's not," she answered. His light brown hair was a tangle from their past moments. It fell in disarray on his forehead and gave him a disheveled but sexy look.

"Good. Don't cut me out of your life, either, just because I proposed and you turned me down. We're going to have to find some common ground because of our baby."

"I know we will and I won't cut you out of my life," she said, feeling a pang because in a lot of ways she liked Sam. How deeply did that liking go? She would return to California. How much would she see him and how would they work out sharing a baby when they lived so far apart?

"If you would prefer a quiet evening here instead of going to the TCC, I'll cook steaks. I promised you a special place—"

"I've really lost my appetite and would just as

soon go home. At the moment, I feel we're at an impasse."

"You need to eat something, Lila. And we can at least talk about sharing this child and how we're going to do so."

She rubbed her head. "Sam, we have six more months before the baby is due. We have a lot of time to think this through and tonight is not a good time for me."

He reached out to take her hand. "I'll take you home if you'll feel better, although I'd prefer you eat something."

"I'm okay. Even that first year, I can't imagine what we'll do because a baby is too little to pass back and forth between us."

"I'll think about it, Lila. You're right about the baby being too small, too young, for him—or her—to be away from you, so I'll have to adapt some way. I'll think about that. Later we can work it out."

"Thank you for being reasonable about it," she said, relieved that he seemed to be willing to co-operate.

"We have the next eighteen or twenty years where we will be involved with each other."

"That's sort of mind-boggling," she said, aware of him seated close beside her.

Still holding her hand, he spread her fingers out over his as he turned his palm up. Her long, slender fingers were smaller than his, her hand smaller.

"Lila, have you seriously thought about being a single parent?"

"Yes, I have. I expected to be a single parent from the first moment I learned I was pregnant," she said.

"I wish you'd been here and I'd been with you," he said solemnly.

"Sorry, Sam. Things are not working out the way you want them to work out."

"So when you go back to California, can I fly out and see where you live?"

"Of course. But do you really see any point in that?"

"If we're sharing a child, I do. I want to know where my child will be."

She gazed into his blue eyes and could feel the

clash of wills and the tension crackling in the air between them. She had never expected them to agree. How could she adjust to dealing with him constantly? He was strong-willed, forceful and accustomed to getting what he wanted. He was also charming, considerate and caring. It was that side of him that was her undoing.

"Yes, you can fly out and see where I live. I'll show you around. I think you'll hate every bit of it. You've grown up here and this is your world. You're so like my dad."

"Thank you. I like your dad and think a lot of him," Sam stated.

"I love my dad, but we have vastly different views on life. He's set in his ways, old-fashioned, chauvinistic, sometimes a little narrow-minded. My family did come to see me once, and after two days they packed and came back home and have not been to California since. Too many people, too much traffic, a big city—all sorts of things that you don't have to put up with in Royal. I expect you'll react like my dad."

"We'll see. I want to be with you when our baby is born," Sam said quietly.

"Let's wait, Sam. What happens if I fall in love with someone before then? Or if you do?"

"I'm not going to fall in love with anyone before that time. Somehow I'm guessing you're not going to, either. You haven't answered my question," he said.

"That's one I want to think about. I imagine the answer will be yes. At least you can come to the hospital. I don't know who I want in the room with me other than the medical people. We'll discuss it later."

"I can wait," he said. "You know your dad will come after me like a tornado sweeping across the prairie when he learns about your pregnancy. He'll want me to marry you and when I tell him I've already proposed and you turned me down, what do you think he'll do?"

"He'll try to get me to marry you every which way he can, but I'm an adult and I learned long ago how to say no to my dad. I'm an adult, and I'm free to do what I want. I'm not worried about Dad. He's a lot of bluster where Hack and I are concerned. He dotes on us. Once he's a grandfather, he'll be so taken with his first grandchild, he won't care what I do."

"I'm not sure I agree with you there."

"Also, he has a chivalrous attitude toward females that keeps him from losing it with me the way he occasionally does with Hack."

"I'm sorry he'll pressure you. No one should be pressured into marriage."

"That's reassuring to hear you say," she said, studying him and thinking it was contradictions like that opinion that kept her drawn to him. "So the subject won't continue to come up between us?"

He turned to look at her, giving her that intense look he could get. "No, it won't," he said as if he had just made a decision about proposing again. "But while you're here in Royal, I want to continue seeing you and going out with you. We have a good time, Lila."

"I don't see any future in seeing each other socially, just more heartache. Besides, I'll be working starting Wednesday and won't have time."

"Scared you'll fall in love with me?" he asked, watching her closely.

"No, I'm not scared," she said. "Well, maybe a little." She rose. "I really would prefer to go home."

He stood, facing her in silence, and again she could feel a tangible clash. "We'll get through this some way. I still want to be with you. I would if you weren't pregnant."

"Sam, you can be so old-fashioned and then turn right around and be so sensible or so much fun or so sexy."

"That's about the best thing you've said tonight."

"At the moment, I think you might as well take me home."

"Sure you don't want to go back to passionate kisses and hot sex?"

She had to smile.

"That's better," he said, touching her chin. "Come on, home it is." He took her hand and they headed to his car.

As they made the drive, he talked, sounding as cheerful as if nothing had happened to ruin his evening. Thankfully, he no longer brought up the subject of marriage or the baby.

"You know there's the annual end-of-summer

after that first night, she had thought about him far more than she had expected she would. But it was this other side to him that made such a difference to her. The past couple of days and the way he had been positive and supportive had caused her to begin to care about him and let down her guard.

Even so, his basic feelings about marriage and about the baby had surfaced and finally, he had acted exactly as she had expected and proposed.

The porch lights were on when they arrived at the Double H. Sam parked in the shadows on the drive beneath a tall oak and when she stepped out, she turned to face him. "Sorry I couldn't say yes, and I regret how the evening turned out, but I really don't have an appetite. I'll get something here soon."

"Take care of yourself and don't worry. Don't get sick over this."

"I won't."

"Lila, let me know when you want to go out and talk."

She nodded. "All right, I will. It might not be on

this trip," she said, feeling as though she was saying goodbye to him in a way—the physical side of their relationship had to stop and it would be easier to walk away now with his views on marriage in the open.

"We can go out and stay off the subject of the future. Just be together."

"I don't see any point," she said, feeling sad. Even though this was what she had expected from the first, it pained her. "The more we go out, the more likely we are to fall in love and I think that might make everything worse, because you're not going to change being an old-fashioned-type guy and I'm not going to change my career," she said.

"Not even to give your baby a daddy who's there all the time?"

"No, I'm not, because I might be happy for a while, but babies grow up and go off to school and then I would be miserable without a career. Better to break this off right now than later because love isn't the total solution."

"Lila, that's a logical answer, but we can go out and just have a good time," he said, wrapping his arm around her waist. "Can't I be more entertaining than you sitting home night after night while you're here? Tonight was less than great for you. I'll go to the TCC on the way home and have a steak. I wish you'd come with me."

"Sorry, not tonight."

"Let me make this night up to you. Darlin', go out with me. I'll pick you up at six again tomorrow and take you somewhere that will make you forget your worries."

Before she could answer, he leaned down to kiss her. His kiss banished her worries. All thinking stopped as she held him and returned his kiss, running her hand across his broad shoulder and then down his back to wrap her arm around his waist, feeling certain she was kissing him goodbye.

He tightened his arms around her, leaning over her to kiss her passionately as if there had not been any argument or discord between them.

When he released her, they both were breathing raggedly. "Will you go out with me tomorrow night?"

"No, I won't, in spite of wanting to kiss you," she whispered, aware every hour spent with him made saying no much more difficult. "We can think about how we'll share our baby, but beyond that, I don't see any reason to go out together."

He put his arm lightly around her waist to walk to the house. "Don't go in and worry, darlin'. Things will work out."

"You're the supreme optimist, Sam."

"It's more fun than being a pessimist—easier, too, because you don't worry as much."

"I don't see either one of us giving up our basic beliefs and hopes and dreams. You want a wife like my mom and I want a career, independence and my California life. Just keep that in mind when you get optimistic and want us to get together," she said as they crossed her wide porch to the front door.

"There is nothing to take your mind off troubles like energetic, sexy dances, some hot kisses and lots of laughs, so if you change your mind about going out, just call me. I don't care what hour it is. I'll drop everything and we'll go."

"I'll bear that offer in mind," she said, hurting, sure they were growing more apart by the minute.

He faced her at the door. "Lila, don't set yourself

up for loneliness and heartbreak. We'll work out everything, darlin'. Go to bed and don't worry." Leaning down, he brushed a light kiss on her mouth. He paused to look into her eyes and she saw a flicker in the depths of his and knew that he would kiss her again. His gaze lowered to her mouth and she couldn't get her breath. In spite of the differences between them, she longed to kiss him. He leaned closer, wrapping his arms around her to draw her up against him while his mouth pressed firmly, kissing her passionately.

When he released her, she opened her eyes to find him watching her. She inhaled deeply. "Your kisses are sinful," she whispered.

"I sort of thought it was your kisses that were so wickedly enticing. Maybe I should try again to see if I'm right."

She stepped back quickly. "Go on to the TCC, Sam, and enjoy your steak. Good night." She hurried into the house and closed the door.

The house was silent, empty downstairs. She was certain her folks were asleep. Moving automatically, she went to her room to get ready for bed while her thoughts were on Sam and his proposal.

She couldn't marry him. There was just no way and it was asking for trouble to go out with him even one more time. But she had already promised to go to the end-of-summer party. He had a way of being cheerful and getting what he wanted. And his farewell with telling her to not worry—how could anyone involved in their situation avoid worrying? Sam was an optimist—and turned a deaf ear when anyone said no to what he wanted. He would soon see she meant it. She hurt and she wanted to get back to her busy life in California, where she could forget Royal, Texas and Sam Gordon. However much in love she was with Sam, she had only to think of his view of women and she could get over all warm feelings for him. Sam Gordon was not the man for her for the rest of her life.

Making an effort to shake Sam out of her thoughts, she focused on the child-care center and Monday's inspection. Another step closer to the finished product. The center had thick walls, insulation, an intercom, closed-circuit cameras, alarm buttons… All sorts of gadgets to keep the children safe in their new center. They needed more money, but she felt sure the club members who supported the children's center would be generous with additional funds.

After taking a warm shower and getting ready for bed, she wandered around her room, pausing at her dresser to open the box from Sam. Light sparkled on the diamonds as she picked up the necklace.

Shaking her head, she returned the locket to the box. Sam was a combination of opposing qualities, some so appealing to her, others not enticing at all. She finally sat in the dark to gaze out the window at the backyard. Lights were on at various spots among the trees and the pool was a glimmering aqua jewel with the pool lights on. What would she do about Sam and how could she deal with him on a long-term basis?

She had no answers except the one certainty— she did not want to marry him. His unexpected behavior over learning about the pregnancy had changed some of her views of him. He wanted this baby beyond her wildest imaginings. His lovemaking had captured more of her heart than before. She knew she was in love with him, but how deep did it run?

He had so many good things about him—he could be kind, gentle, understanding, amazing in his attitude about the baby, fun, sexier than anyone she had ever known, optimistic and confident. She had a wonderful time with him always, until they got on the subject of her career and the other side of him popped up—chauvinistic, old-fashioned, stubborn. A take-charge, commanding man who didn't know how to accept not getting his way. Sometimes Sam's charming qualities outweighed the ones she didn't like—not just sometimes, most of the time.

She had to admit, she had some strong feelings for him and in too many ways she liked him a lot. What scared her most—Sam was turning into a true friend. If she really had a problem, she could tell him and trust him. Friendship: the strongest base for love.

"Sam," she whispered. "Sam Gordon, my friend, my lover, father of my child. You already have my heart." She didn't want him to, but she ached so badly she suspected he did, almost completely, but not quite enough to give up her independence, her career, the way of life she wanted.

Finally she climbed into bed to dream about Sam and being in his arms.

Monday morning she dressed in designer jeans with a bright red shirt that covered her waist to hide her pregnancy. How much easier this would be away from Royal.

Her cell phone rang. When she answered, she heard Shannon.

"Lila, Amanda Battle called me a few minutes ago because Nathan got a call from Gil Addison. There was an inspection scheduled today for the alarm system for the new center."

"Yes, I remember. We're moving right along."

"The inspection failed. After they got to checking on it, they said someone had tampered with it."

Nine

A chill turned Lila to ice. Her first thought was Sam. He had been so totally opposed to the child-care center and still opposed it. Sam had been at the club late Sunday night. In addition to his op-position, he was in construction and a member of the TCC. He would know how to get into the alarm system. He was a take-charge person ac-customed to getting his way. Could Sam have been the one?

She doubled her fist against her heart because she hurt over the thought that Sam might do such a thing. It would be a betrayal of trust, besides being unlawful.

"Do they have a clue who did it?" She closed her eyes, hoping she would not hear Sam's name.

"Not that I know about. Nathan's over there looking into it. Nathan is a smart man. He'll catch who did this. They've already said it had to be a TCC member because no one else would have access to that room or the center's alarm system unless it was the staff, and they aren't at the club on weekend nights except for the security guard."

"There are a lot of members who opposed the center, including my dad. My dad would never willfully destroy part of the club just to cause trouble. Dad is law-abiding. You'd think all the TCC members would be," Lila said.

"I'm sure. It's terrible because friends will be accusing friends. The vandalism goes against all the club stands for," Lila said, thinking again of Sam and Josh Gordon. "My folks can account for their whereabouts last night. They went to bed early and were here asleep when I got home."

"Don't worry, Lila. I don't think anyone will accuse your dad, and definitely not your mom. I don't have a worry where she's concerned and I don't think it was a woman. This seems more like the work of one of the men who is bitter over women being allowed in and now, the last straw, having a child-care center."

"I agree. It'll be someone in that group. I hope Nathan finds him.

"Shannon, my dad, Sam and Josh Gordon, all of those men who fought so bitterly, they empowered the person who did this. That fight and the hard feelings afterward may be what pushed someone into this," she said, thinking Sam couldn't have done it. Basically, she thought he was really a good person, just had old-fashioned ways. Her first fears about him were gone.

"I imagine you're right. The person who did it is probably friends with those who opposed the center and thinks he was doing them all a favor. I'll see you later this morning. Are you still meeting with that rancher about the filming?"

"Bob Milton. Not until one o'clock. That won't interfere with us. About the alarm, do you wonder what else the person might do?"

"We may have more vandalism with the children's center."

"Between this and Alex's puzzling disappearance, some bad things are happening. And this last event means someone intends to prevent the center from opening."

"I hate to leave Royal with a disaster hitting the children's center, but Rory and I have plans. Anyway, I'll see you at eleven at the club. Bye, Lila."

Lila set her cell phone on the dresser and rubbed her forehead.

For the short time she had thought Sam might have sabotaged the alarm, she had more hurt than anger. There could only be one reason that the result was hurt. She had fallen in love with him.

Feeling forlorn and unhappy, she covered her face. She was in love and it was impossible. His attitude about the baby and her pregnancy had amazed her and won her heart, yet she was still torn, now more than ever, over his old-fashioned views, his determination to marry even though he wasn't in love with her.

A TCC member had vandalized the alarm—that went against all the club stood for. Who could have done such a thing? Her doubts about Sam were gone. He wouldn't do that any more than her dad would. But she still felt their arguments and bitter feelings had given resolve to whoever did it. The vandal may have thought the others would be supportive if he ever got caught.

In a way they couldn't foresee, with their bitter fight over the center, those men had inadvertently contributed to what had happened.

This just brought back into focus Sam's views and old-fashioned ways.

She had no control over her heart. She loved Sam and she was going to have to get over it. Moving mindlessly, she headed toward the kitchen.

She found her mother still in her blue velvet robe, lingering over her coffee. Her mom's stylish bob was neatly combed. Except for a slight frown, she looked her usual serene self.

"Hi. I guess you've heard the news about the TCC," Lila said, pouring a glass of orange juice.

"Yes, and I can't believe it. Even your dad, who definitely opposes the child-care center, was shocked and upset. It worries him most that it has to be a TCC member."

"I'm sure that will be a big concern to a lot of them. For a few minutes I wondered about Sam."

"Sam would never do something like that," Barbara said, and Lila shook her head.

"I don't think he would, but some TCC member did this. Sam was bitterly against the center but says he's not opposed to it any longer."

"Sam's a good man, Lila."

"I know he is. I need to get ready. I'm meeting Shannon at the club."

Lila went back to her room and stood there thinking about the failed inspection. She couldn't stand worrying about it all day.

As she drove into town, she was angry that one of the men would stoop to trying to sabotage the efforts to get a child-care center open in the club. She barely glanced at the familiar surroundings.

As she crossed the parking lot, Sam climbed out of his car and turned to greet her.

He wore a dark brown suit and a lighter brown tie and as always, the sight of him affected her physically, giving her heart a jump. He looked handsome, cheerful, friendly, a side of him that conflicted with his determination, self-will and authoritative manner.

"Have you heard about the child-care center?" she asked without preamble.

His eyes narrowed a fraction as he placed his hands on his hips, pushing open his coat. "Yes, I have. Too bad, but that can be fixed without a major setback. It's a temporary interference."

Taking a deep breath, she watched him intently. "I know you have opposed the center from the beginning and argued to keep it from being accepted. You, my dad, a lot of others. The bitter campaign may have given this person the feeling he had the support of all of you."

Sam's blue eyes became glacial as he placed his hands on her shoulders. "Damn, Lila, when we argued against having the center, that was just democracy. I've opposed women in the club. I've opposed the children's center. But there is no way in hell I would condone a criminal act."

She gazed into his eyes and saw the anger. She was beginning to learn that Sam did not hide his emotions. His face was expressive, and he made no effort to keep people from learning how he felt. And right now he looked like a man telling the truth.

"You know, they say it has to be a club member," she said.

"I know, and that's depressing. I would have thought all the members were above that sort of thing."

She knew he wouldn't destroy property. Sam was smart enough, too, to know it wouldn't stop the center from opening.

"Lila, let me take you to dinner tonight. I've missed seeing you," he said.

Regret filled her as she shook her head. "Thank you, but there's just no point in pursuing a relationship. You have your views and your ways. You're an old-fashioned man with ideas about women and what you'd want in a wife. Our lives don't fit together. Thanks, anyway. I'm meeting Shannon." She walked past him.

He caught up and held the door for her.

"Maybe you don't know me as well as you think you do, Lila."

"I know what's important to me. Bye."

She walked away and he let her go. Her back prickled, but she didn't glance around.

Sam walked into one of the empty lounges and

closed the door. He wanted a moment to think about Lila. Looking out the window without really seeing anything, he thought about Lila's accusations of being chauvinistic, old-fashioned, even more about her earlier declarations that he didn't love her.

Why couldn't she see that love could develop between them? He wanted to be with her. He wanted her in his bed every night. If she would move back to Royal, move in with him, marry him, he was certain love would come.

He shook his head. She would never move back to Royal. He had no doubts about that. The minute she had gone to college, she never looked back. Was she right? Were the differences between them too great?

How important was she to him? That was the question.

Restless, Sam stood and walked to the window. He had sent flowers, taken Lila out, but he hadn't realized that the gulf between them might be permanent.

He wasn't in love and she definitely wasn't, but they were good together. The sex was fabulous and now they had a baby on the way. With or without love, they should get married, but she would never change her mind or settle for the life he would want his wife to have.

If she felt that way, pretty flowers or dinners out would not change her mind. It had to be a lot deeper than that.

Was he making a mistake, being too old-fashioned in wanting to get married? Was it a mistake to marry without love? He had been so sure love would come, but what if he was wrong? Was he trying to tie himself into a relationship that would make them both unhappy? He didn't want a wife who was an ambitious career woman. He didn't want a wife who lived in California while he lived in Texas.

He didn't see how love could come without really getting to know each other. And with Lila, that would mean a long-term relationship, which wasn't going to happen with him in Royal and her in California. In two days she would be working and he wouldn't see her. In a few weeks she would go to California and he probably wouldn't see her until Christmas, if then.

He clenched his fists and thought about their baby. A baby needed a family. Maybe it was an old-fashioned notion, but he felt that with his whole being.

He was going to have to let go. Lila would share their baby, but he needed to face reality. Lila wasn't the woman for him. She didn't want to change and he didn't want to change. The differences between them were huge.

His decision brought him no peace. He hurt and he missed her. "You'll get over this," he said aloud to himself, knotting his fists and taking a deep breath. "Forget her."

How long would it take to get over her? How long would it be before she didn't occupy his thoughts through his waking hours? With a baby on the way, it seemed impossible to think he could forget her. She was going to be the mother of his child. However long it took, he was going to have to let her go.

When the movie people arrived Wednesday morning and Lila vanished from his life, Sam told himself it was for the best. Twice he couldn't

resist calling her. Most of her work was in surrounding counties and the only contact he had
with her was a brief snatch of conversation.

The second time when she answered her phone,
she sounded breathless. "Sam, I really can't talk.
They're ready to shoot a scene and they had a
quick huddle about it and decided they wanted
the child in the scene, so I have to find a child's
bed, either an old-time wooden one or iron, pref-
erably iron."

"Can I get it for you?" he said, heading toward
the parking lot and his car in case she said yes.

"There's one store outside of Royal—Buttons
& Bows, sort of a flea market. They're looking
through their stuff and will call me back. There's
one on the highway to Midland I'm going to look
at. I'm sorry I can't talk, but someone is driving
me and I'm calling places. I'll get back with you
later."

"Sure, Lila," he said, knowing she would not
and he would not call her again.

A week later, his first reaction was surprise
when she called him at his office. His heart
skipped a beat at the sound of her voice and he

gripped his cell phone tightly as if he could hang on to her.

"Sam, sorry to interrupt your business day. I have a request. The director would like to meet you and I wondered if we could possibly come by your office briefly this afternoon? We should be finished by six—would that be too late?"

His pulse jumped and all he could think about was seeing Lila. "Whatever time you want will be fine. My appointments were earlier, so I'm free. Josh isn't here this afternoon."

"Doesn't matter. Roddy just wants to meet you because of the hotel in Amarillo that you built."

"Would you rather take him to the TCC?"

"Not really. I think he will enjoy seeing your office," she said, talking faster than usual, and he suspected she would end the conversation soon and get back to work. "He isn't friendly with strangers, but he was impressed by the hotel you built in Amarillo because on his first trip to Texas he stayed there. His name is Rodman Parkeson. He's a little brisk and abrupt—I'm warning you now. He's thinking about building a new house in California and I think he wants to talk to you about construction. We won't take much of your time."

"You can have all my time you want, Lila," Sam said, unable to keep a hoarse note out of his voice. "I've missed you." He was telling himself to let go, yet wanted her badly.

"Thank you," she replied briskly, making him wonder if she was with other people or really didn't care. "See you around six."

She was gone and he missed her. He didn't want her going back to California soon. He thought about the end-of-summer party at the TCC—that would be his last time with her, perhaps for a long time. He rubbed his forehead, hating to think about her leaving Texas yet telling himself it was for the best. When would he stop hurting over her?

He got up, moving chairs slightly in his office, pausing to look around and think how it would appear to a stranger. The dark oak walls still appealed to him and his hand-carved walnut desk was free of clutter. He wandered through the reception area and outside, standing on the porch.

The redbrick Greek Revival building was on a

large shady lot. He and Josh had built it to look like a gracious Southern mansion, but it was a practical office that met their needs. The front porch had rocking chairs and the yard held beds of multicolored flowers. A redbrick walk ran from the parking lot to the front door.

Behind the office were the workings of the construction company with steel sheds for lumber, metal buildings for equipment. There was a garage for trucks and another building for the machinery.

The day seemed twice as long as usual, but finally at six his phone rang and Lila said they were on the office porch.

Sam strode out the front door, taking a deep breath at the sight of her. With her hair twisted and pinned up behind her head, she looked more businesslike. She wore navy slacks and a sleeveless matching blouse with navy pumps. All his intentions to forget her and get over her vanished. He wanted to wrap his arms around her and kiss her. Instead, he offered his hand. "Lila," he said, gazing into her wide green eyes, which told him nothing about her feelings.

Her hand was warm, dainty, and he hated to release her. "Sam, I want you to meet Roddy Parkeson. Roddy, meet Sam Gordon, half owner of Gordon Construction."

With an effort, Sam tore his attention from Lila to extend his hand to a stocky man with thick curly brown hair streaked with gray. His dark brown eyes were sharp and alert. He gripped Sam's hand briefly in a solid, quick handshake. "I'm happy to meet you," he said, looking around. "This office is as fantastic as your hotel. I was enjoying myself looking at this porch. This is marvelous—a beautiful addition to the town."

"Thank you. Feel free to look all you want. If you'd like, I'll show you inside."

"I'd like that. My dad was in construction and I worked in it off and on when I was a kid," Roddy said while Sam held the door for Lila and Roddy and they entered the cool lobby. Sam guessed the director to be in his forties, and he was short enough that Sam could easily see the top of his head. Roddy's nose was crooked as if broken sometime in his past and Sam noticed thick hands that looked as rough as some of the local cowboys'.

"My dad was hired to work in the film business, so that's where I've always been, but I can recognize sound construction and I know the kind of architecture and buildings that I like," he continued as Sam directed them to his office. "That hotel you built in Amarillo was excellent. And this is a fantastic office. I'm from L.A., but I had a great-aunt who lived in Natchez, Mississippi. How I loved those homes."

Sam nodded, wondering whether he had heard Lila correctly when she had said Rodman Parkeson was brisk and abrupt. He had talked constantly since being introduced. Sam looked at Lila, who smiled faintly. As Roddy circled the room talking about construction and looking at crown molding and the hardwood floor, Lila leaned close and whispered, "You're a hit."

Sam didn't answer. He crossed the room and tried to focus on Roddy's conversation, finding it difficult to take his gaze away from Lila.

Roddy spent an hour looking at the Gordon office and sitting on the porch talking to Sam and Lila.

"If you have time, Roddy, we could drive out to

my home. I can grill some dinner and show you my house if you want to look at more construction, or we can just sit and talk over Texas steaks."

"Texas steaks and your home would be great," Roddy said, standing.

The evening was enjoyable while at the same time frustrating because Sam wanted Lila to himself. When they finally headed for her car, they stood on the drive talking for another twenty minutes before Roddy walked around to the passenger side and climbed inside.

"You were really a big hit with him. He doesn't usually talk to strangers or take time like this when he's away on a job. Thanks, Sam, for all your hospitality."

"A nice guy," Sam said. "We still have a date for the end-of-the-summer party."

"Yes, we do. Night, Sam, and thanks again."

He opened the door for her and closed it when she was seated. Stepping back, he watched them drive away. "So much for trying to forget her," he said under his breath. If he married her, this was the way his life would be—watching her drive away to go back to her career. He didn't want that life, but he couldn't stop wanting her.

"Dammit," he said, kicking a pebble with the toe of his boot.

To his relief, finally the last Thursday of August came. As suddenly as the film people had come, they left Texas to return to California. Lila would fly out Monday morning and be gone. Each time he thought of her leaving Texas, his insides clutched. He hurt, and the knowledge that he needed to get over it didn't diminish the feeling of loss.

Sam called Lila to ask her to dinner Thursday night. "Lila, I've had time to think about all you've said and I've had a chance to see how demanding your career is. I think we need to talk."

Ten

Lila's heart missed a beat. Sam's voice was solemn, different from his usual cheerful self. "Then it will be a good thing to talk," she said, wondering if he finally had realized marriage would never work.

"I'll pick you up at seven," he said and then was gone.

She replaced the phone and felt a squeeze to her heart. At the same time, she nodded. "Finally, Sam," she whispered.

She dressed carefully, a simple sleeveless navy dress that fastened beneath her chin and had a straight skirt that went to midcalf. A conservative dress she usually wore to work. She had the feeling that Sam might be ready to tell her good-bye, which should make her feel relieved instead of empty and dreading the dinner with him.

When she stepped into the living room to wait for Sam, her mother walked by, saw her and came into the room. "It'll be nice to see Sam again."

Lila ran her finger along a table. "Mom, I think this is goodbye for us."

"Lila, it won't be goodbye. You are going to be parents, and for years Sam will be part of your life."

"Not a major part," she said.

"Think carefully, honey. Sam is a fine person."

"I know. And he wants a wife just like you. I'm not that woman. Speaking of," she said, seeing Sam drive up. "I'll go on out. I might as well get this over with."

"Lila, make sure you don't want Sam to be a major part of your life. Be very sure of what you're doing."

"I'm really sure," she said, knowing this was definitely for the best. "The hurt will go away," she whispered. She walked out to get into his car, hoping to get seated before he was really out, but he had already walked around and he held open the passenger door. Her heart thudded at the sight of him. He looked more handsome than ever in his charcoal suit, white dress shirt and red tie. Her determination to tell him goodbye made her hurt even more. One look at Sam's face and she knew it would be goodbye tonight. He had a somber expression she had never seen, a hard, angry look.

"I have reservations at Willow Hollow. I thought we might see fewer people we know and have fewer interruptions."

"That's fine," she replied, relieved they weren't staying in Royal where they would see friends all through the evening. Willow Hollow was in a neighboring county and was an excellent restaurant, but she had lost her appetite again, which had been happening more and more, lately. He closed the car door and she watched him walk around and climb in.

"Are you resting up a little from the work?" he asked after they were on the highway.

"I suppose. That and packing up to get ready to return to California on Monday."

How polite they were with each other. She felt a rift between them as if Sam had put a wall around himself, which was totally unlike him. She should have felt intensely relieved, but so far the feeling hadn't happened.

"I got a call today from Roddy."

"Oh, really? Did he have a construction question?"

"Sort of. He offered me a job and suggested I think about moving my business to California."

Shocked, she stared at Sam and then she laughed and shook her head. "Roddy can be so cold to people he doesn't know. He was bowled over by your work. What a compliment, Sam. I know you have no interest—what kind of job did he offer you?"

"He wants me to build his new home," Sam said, smiling for the first time that evening.

"Oh, for heaven's sake! I knew he had talked about having a home built, but he lives in a very nice mansion. I bet he wants you to build him some kind of Georgian or Colonial or Greek Revival, something like his great-aunt's house or one of those in Mississippi."

"You're right. I thanked him. The offer was flattering and he also has a film project he wanted to hire me to do. He made a big sales pitch, which was very flattering."

"Roddy? I can't imagine. He's used to ordering people around and pushing them into doing things. What kind of sales pitch?"

"How great my construction company would be in L.A."

"That's probably true. Have you told Josh?"

"I will. He'll just give me one of his looks and go on to the next thing on the agenda."

"I'm surprised, but that's very complimentary. Wow. You really impressed Roddy. He does know construction. His dad had a successful business."

"Roddy is a nice man."

She laughed and shook her head. "He must really want you to build his house. He could hire you anyway and you could work on his house from Texas."

"Actually, he talked about that, but I don't think that would work. I'm not into flying back and forth."

She thought about their baby and wondered how they would ever work out sharing a child. That sobering thought made her forget Roddy and ride in silence until they were at the restaurant.

She was barely aware of the linen-covered tables, the dahlias in crystal vases on each table, the candlelight and soft music. All she could see was the handsome man across from her, the father of her baby, the man she was somewhat in love with. For the first time, his smile and the sparkle in his blue eyes were gone.

She ordered tomato basil soup. He ordered his usual steak and as soon as they were alone, he took her hand. "I've thought over all you've said. I've thought about our future," he said, and her heart dropped. "What may be most important, I stood on the sidelines as the movie was filming. While I didn't see you at work, I learned a little about your job and your hours. I finally listened and thought about all you've said to me and I have to agree with you. You're right, Lila," he said.

These were words she had thought she wanted to hear, so why did they cut like a knife to her heart?

"We're not wildly, deeply in love with each other," he continued in a somber tone.

His declaration hurt more than everything else. She had said the same thing to him, but when he said it, the words stung badly. A knot came in her throat and she tried to fight back tears, aggravated at herself for reacting this way when he was merely echoing her own sentiments.

"I want a wife who is home with my children. Maybe that is old-fashioned and chauvinistic, but that's the way I am. A lot of people don't have a choice, but I'm fortunate to have been successful enough that my wife can afford to do that and that's what I want. Call it selfish—I can't see it that way. You want to work and pursue a career. You're very ambitious, very independent and you don't need me and the kind of man I am in your life."

She looked down and tried to control her emotions. She needed to answer him. He was silent, and she was certain he waited for her agreement, but she was scared if she met his gaze or tried to answer him, she would burst into tears. What was the matter with her?

Knotting her hands in her lap, she looked up. "I'm glad you realize that, Sam. We're friends and we both like each other, but it isn't real love. This is the sensible thing and we'll work out life for our baby."

"After the first year, I'd like equal time. Actually, with your folks in Royal and with me being close friends with them, I think they'll be happy for me to have our baby a lot of the time."

"Half?" she said, frowning. She had never imagined having to give up her baby half the time. "We'll work it out," she said with a long sigh. Sam could be exactly right about her folks. "I'm glad you see this," she said, barely able to get out the words and looking down at her fingers locked together in her lap. "We will work it all out. We still have some time before this baby's birth."

"When will you tell the rest of your family? I want to be ready for your dad."

"I'm telling him before I get on the plane Monday. I can't live with him otherwise."

She looked up and Sam frowned slightly. "You don't look happy. I just did what you've wanted all along."

"I do want that. We were never meant for each

other. It's just a hard decision and I like you. We've had a great time together and you're a friend."

He gazed at her solemnly and said, "I hope to hell we're not making a big mistake."

"Think about my career and you'll get back on track."

He looked away and inhaled deeply. When he turned back to face her, he looked more composed. "You're right. All I have to do is think about how you've been working fourteen or so hours each day lately. That brings me back to reality."

They became silent as the waitstaff delivered their dinners. After several sips of her soup, she felt she couldn't get down another bite. She looked at Sam to see he wasn't eating either.

"Isn't your steak all right?"

"The steak is fine. I've lost my appetite. We're being sensible, Lila, but all I really want to do is take you to bed with me."

"If you're not going to eat and I'm not going to eat, I think we should just go home. We've said what we needed to and it's time to move on," she declared flatly, hurting more than ever over his last statement. She wanted to be in his arms, she wanted his kisses and lovemaking, to flirt with him, but this was the only way and they weren't making a mistake. She would get over him. She had to.

On the way home they talked about inconsequential things and the whole time she tried to avoid thinking about the evening or what he had said. In a few days she would return to California and they wouldn't talk, maybe until Thanksgiving. It was finally over with him except to work out custody. Half the time. He wanted custody and he might be right about her parents wanting their grandchild in Royal often. Thinking what a muddle she had made of her life, she rubbed her forehead. For a moment she half expected Sam to reach over and touch her, to reassure her the way he had before, but he concentrated on driving and rode in silence.

At the ranch he walked her to the door. "Goodbye, Lila. I know it isn't really goodbye, but in a way it is. We'll share a baby but not much else. I will work with you, but sooner or later we can start going through our lawyers. I'll marry someday and have a family I can be a daddy for all the time and a wife who's there for me and our kids. You'll have your life. I'll still be a dad for our baby, too. I won't give up on my child even if we are halfway across the country from each other."

"I know you won't," she whispered, fighting tears more than ever. "We'd better cancel the date for Saturday night."

"Sure. Seems pointless now."

"Goodbye, Sam." She hurried inside.

To her relief, no one was around. She rushed to her room and closed the door. The tears came and she couldn't understand her reaction. Sam had finally agreed with her, done just what she wanted, so why did it hurt so badly and seem so incredibly wrong? She had a wonderful career she loved and she couldn't come back and settle in Royal, marry Sam and only do volunteer work, but at the moment California loomed as a lonely place. Once she was back in her own home and could walk on the beach and see the ocean, when she was back in the routine of work, back with her friends, she would feel differently.

"Sam," she whispered. "If only you weren't so old-fashioned…."

* * *

Friday morning she waited to go to breakfast until she knew her dad would be out of the house and more than likely her brother would still be asleep. Her mother was still in the kitchen and turned to study her. "I take it you and Sam won't be going out tonight."

"No. He finally has realized we aren't suited for marriage."

"I'm sorry, Lila. Want to go shopping? What would you like to eat?"

"I have a lunch appointment today, Mom, but thanks. Maybe tomorrow morning. I'm not really hungry."

"Eat something, Lila, so you don't get sick. You'll feel better. You can go with us to the TCC tomorrow to the end-of-summer party. You won't go with Sam now, will you?"

"No, I won't."

"It's a fun evening and you'll enjoy it. They'll have an open house in the new child-care center with tours for those who are interested."

Lila thought about the previous night and how little she and Sam had even talked to each other.

She poured orange juice and got a muffin, picking up the paper and sitting at the table to try to eat a little and to try to stop thinking about Sam. Did he give her any thought or had he picked up and gone on with his life?

Sam showered and shaved, getting dressed for the day. In the midmorning he had an appointment at the TCC. This afternoon he had a house to look at. He hadn't slept and he still thought about Lila and missed her, but he expected that to diminish. He felt a pang and tried to think about her job, her damnable career that he couldn't deal with.

He was scheduled to meet with a client at the TCC and they would talk about business over lunch. He had reserved a meeting room and ordered lunch brought in so they could keep working in privacy without interruption.

Sam talked to his secretary and left, driving the short distance to the Texas Cattleman's Club.

He was meeting Tom Devlin, another TCC member. With his thoughts on Lila, Sam parked at the club and stepped into the cool front. He saw one of the signs that carried the TCC motto and had hung near the entrance for as long as he could remember.

Some member wasn't true to the motto, Leadership, Justice, Peace, or was it misguided loyalty that had caused someone to tamper with the alarm system in the children's center? Had the person thought they would be doing a favor by delaying the center from opening?

The alarm system had already been repaired. The center would hold an open house the night of the party, so the tampering really had no long-term effect. Someone was shortsighted or maybe just angry enough to want to cause trouble even when it did not stop progress.

As Sam passed the dining room, he glanced inside. All his breath left him as he gazed across the busy room and saw Lila having coffee with a man Sam didn't know. He felt as if a fist had punched him in the middle. The man was in boots, slacks and a Western shirt. A broad-brimmed Western hat was on an empty chair. The man laughed at something Lila said and Sam felt another twist to his insides.

Who was she seeing? The man was a stranger,

but Lila had to be having a wonderful time with him. In minutes, Lila laughed. Sam realized how he was staring and moved out of the doorway, stepping down the hall, wanting to go back and look at them again. She was bound to go out with other men, but he hadn't expected it this soon. He hadn't expected her to date while she was carrying his baby.

Who was the man? How serious was she? It had to be a casual meeting.

Sam went to his appointment and for the first half hour tried to concentrate but could not focus on what Tom was saying. He tried all through the appointment and it finally finished. As soon as Sam was alone, he gathered papers and put them in a briefcase. As he left, he walked past the center, the billiard room and the dining room, but Lila was nowhere to be seen.

"Hi, Sam," Beau Hacket said, shaking hands with Sam. "You've sent Lila a lot of flowers this summer. Rather impressive."

Sam didn't care to discuss his and Lila's relationship with Beau. "I thought I saw her here earlier."

"Oh, yeah. Earlier she had lunch with some friends and then she met with one of those ranchers to thank him for allowing the film company to shoot part of the movie on his ranch. It was Bob Milton. No telling where Lila is now. She does her own thing."

Relief swamped Sam and he let out his breath. Suddenly the day had brightened and he could think about something besides Lila. He talked a few more minutes to Beau.

"I was sorry to hear about the alarm system failing the inspection. I think it upset Lila," Sam said, beginning to decide that Beau knew little about his daughter at this point.

"I'm sure it would, but her heart is in California and that job of hers. And she knew the alarm would be fixed and pass inspection. Frankly, I don't think it was a smart thing to do, but what's worrisome is it had to be one of us. That's what's bad."

"I agree."

"Probably all of us who voted against the center are suspects. I've already talked to Nathan, and I think he is talking to each member. There's no way to know everyone who voted against the center."

"You're right. I hope they catch the culprit quickly. It's good to see you, Beau."

"Good to see you, Sam," he said as they shook hands again.

Sam walked away feeling enormously better, in euphoria until he was in his car and then he sat still with shock. To hurt so badly and be as upset as he had been over seeing Lila with another man, how strong were his feelings for her? Had he already fallen in love with her and hadn't realized his own feelings?

Stunned, he sat in the parking lot staring into space again while the question consumed him. Was he already deeply in love with Lila? If he was, could he let her go out of his life? Could he let another man try to win her heart and take her away forever? If he truly and deeply loved her, how could he win her heart? How much would he have to change his life—and could he change?

Deep in thought, questioning his own emotions, he replayed the morning. His thoughts skipped to the times they were together and their love-making.

He had already realized that he had never dated another woman like her. She could excite him more, entertain him more, be a friend. He just plain enjoyed being with her. He had wanted her in his bed at night—every night—since that first time together, but he had tried to cool down that wish.

Was he in love and hadn't even realized it?

And if in love with her, how could he let her go?

Lila was absolutely the epitome of the independent woman. Could he adjust to her need for a career? How would he ever convince her he loved her? He couldn't win her over with flowers or diamonds or proposals. How could he let her know that he would support her projects as well as his own?

He thought about Roddy's sales pitch to move his business to California. It had seemed absurd at first, but then Roddy had wanted him to build a mansion and work on a movie project. If he moved to Los Angeles, he would have contacts through Roddy. Could he leave Royal? How deep did his love run for Lila? Was it deep enough to change his whole way of life and his most basic beliefs?

In love with Lila. How had she captured his heart? One night of lust should not make him fall in love with her. Yet it had. From the first, looking back, he loved her. He had never been able to get her out of his thoughts after that first night.

Astounded by his own reactions, he continued to sit in his parked car while he thought about his feelings for Lila.

He loved her—now if he could just convince her that he did. And change her opinion of him, because she would never fall in love with him as long as she saw him as old-fashioned and chauvinistic.

How could he alter Lila's view of him? The question plagued him and he had no answer.

He pulled out his phone to call her. The minute he heard her voice, his grip tightened on his phone. "Lila, it's Sam. If you're free, I still want to take you to the TCC end-of-summer party. We shouldn't part the way we did and I need to see you."

Eleven

When Saturday arrived, eager anticipation hummed in Sam as he dressed. He would be with her again. He wouldn't think about her leaving on Monday.

The party was at the TCC and it was casual with the pool open. There would be swimming, dancing, food, contests, games and billiards. They were showing the new child-care center and Gil had announcements. The end-of-summer party had always been fun, with plenty of things for kids so whole families could attend.

Hurrying because he was anxious to see Lila, Sam walked to the door of the Double H to pick her up. Afterward, he intended to talk her into staying the night at his place.

He rang the bell, expecting to see Mrs. Hacket, who usually welcomed him.

Instead, the door swung open and Lila stood there gazing solemnly at him. The sight of her made his heart pound.

Lila faced Sam and opened the door, inviting him in. In jeans, boots and a short-sleeved Western shirt, he looked handsome, breathtaking, and longing squeezed her heart. She wanted to walk into his arms and forget all their differences, but she couldn't.

Instead, she greeted him and kept her distance. "I'm ready to go, Sam. Mom and Dad are still inside and Mom is running late. She said for us to go on ahead."

"I won't argue that one," he said, taking Lila's arm as she called goodbye to her parents, closing the door behind her.

He held her hands, still facing her and blocking her way. "You look gorgeous tonight. Thursday night was no way to part. Lila, all I want to do is pull you into my arms and kiss you."

A thrill rocked her even when she didn't want it to. "Sam, I thought we had settled all this," she said, wondering if going to the party with him was going to be a mistake. She would leave Monday for California and she didn't plan to return to Royal until Thanksgiving. By then she hoped all the longing and desire she felt for Sam would be gone. They had no future and she was determined to reconcile herself to that.

Walking to his car, he took her hand. The August sun was still high as Sam drove away from the Hacket ranch.

"You're quiet tonight," he said, taking her hand to place it on his thigh as he drove.

His thigh was muscled, firm, warm through the denim. She looked at Sam's profile and thought about telling him goodbye. She thought about her doctor's visit. She wasn't ready to break that news to Sam. On highly personal matters, it seemed easier to postpone revealing anything to him. Especially news she was struggling to cope with herself. He might try to stop her from flying out Monday and she had to get back to her job.

"You're quiet tonight, Lila."

"It's been busy for two weeks. It's nice to sit and relax."

"After the party we can go to my place and I'll help you relax," he said, glancing at her with a smile.

She shook her head. "Sorry, Sam. After the party I need to go home."

"We haven't really had a chance to talk a lot or make plans."

"We don't need to plan yet. We'll get to plans later when it's not so emotional between us. We both agreed to back off."

He nodded and a muscle worked in his jaw.

"Sam, we would never really be happy together. You saw a little of what my job is like—the demands on my time."

"Yes, I did. Tonight let's forget jobs and futures." He glanced at her as he drove. "Okay?"

"Yes." When she started to move her hand from his thigh, he placed it right back.

"I want you touching me. I've been counting the hours until tonight."

"You have so many women following you

around, you can't be counting hours until you're with me."

"Oh, yes, I have, and I think you exaggerate. Besides, I shooed them away because I only have eyes for one redhead with big green eyes. A redhead whose kisses set me on fire," he added in a husky tone.

"We basically said goodbye Thursday night. Stop flirting. Habit that it is—stop. Don't make me regret coming with you."

"I'm resourceful, darlin'. Tonight I have all kinds of plans."

She studied him, wondering what he had planned. When they drove into the club's parking lot, there were already a lot of cars. A valet took Sam's key while Sam linked his arm through hers and they entered the club.

"I wish Shannon could be here tonight, but she's gone back to Austin. The other women will be here. I haven't seen the center for two weeks now."

"Come on. We'll look where our baby will be sometime," he said.

Our baby—Sam was playing on her emotions and she didn't know which was worse, the frosty silence they'd had Thursday night or his flirting and touching, because all of it tore her up.

They walked down the hall and turned into what had once been the billiard room. Lila gasped. "Would you look at this. My goodness," she said, looking around a room with colorful walls and bright colors on small chairs and tables. She glanced at built-in shelves and cabinets. In one corner were two deep sinks secured to the wall at a child's level. "Look, the sinks are in the paint area." Unopened boxes were stacked in various parts of the room. On the opposite wall from where she was standing, she saw a new wide door, plus two new big windows with a view of where the new playground would go. Late-afternoon sunlight streamed through both windows.

Other members and guests walked through the center, greeted by some of the women members.

"They have the door to the outside," Lila noticed.

"That's all. The playground hasn't been started," Sam said, looking through a window.

"This is wonderful in here." She smiled at him. "I guess I'm more excited about it than you."

"I think it's great and they're a little ahead of schedule. They need to raise more money to finish—Gil will talk about that briefly tonight."

"I hope they can. Surely they'll be able to with this group, unless too many oppose it still."

Sam merely smiled at her and she wondered if he hoped they had difficulty raising the money.

"I'm so impressed." She turned to walk back through the center while Sam followed her into the hall, switching off lights and leaving open the door.

"I hear music somewhere. Let's go dance," he said.

In minutes they were dancing to a fast number and she moved around Sam, glad to let go and have fun, relieved to dance after a grueling two weeks and the emotional upheaval of Thursday night.

She watched Sam dance, twisting his narrow hips, making sexy moves, and she remembered his long legs entangled with hers after loving. She ached with wanting him. She loved him, but she intended to get over her feelings for him.

She watched him, moved with him. Desire simmered, heating her, making her think about love-making.

Later, in a slow dance, Sam held her close. "I missed you these past two weeks. I don't want you to go off like that again."

"Sorry, but we've settled all this. We go our separate ways and we'll both be happier and better off. You'll see," she said, wishing she could feel certain that's what would happen.

"I wish I could keep you here," he said.

Startled, she looked up at him and shook her head. "That's out of the question. I go back to my California life."

"This is good, Lila," he said softly, slow-dancing with her, holding her against him, and for a few minutes she closed her eyes and stopped thinking about when they would part.

As they danced in the large ballroom, the music stopped. Gil Addison called for order. "Welcome," he said, and received applause and cheers in return.

He motioned for quiet. "This is our end-of-summer party, although I don't think the weather knows it's the end of summer in Royal because it's still mighty hot. We have a big evening planned with games, hot dogs, burgers and prizes." He paused for applause and cheers. "And lots of cold beer and dancing." There was more applause.

"As all of you know, I'm sure, we've voted in a new child-care center, which has progressed nicely." He waited again while applause rose until he waved his hand and quiet resumed.

"We recently had a break-in and the alarm system was tampered with, causing a temporary setback in meeting the construction deadline. So far, no word on the identity of the person who tampered with the system, which brings me to an announcement. That catastrophe had not been budgeted. Also, a playground was suggested and voted in earlier this month. We need to raise funds for all of this. Any donations will be happily accepted. You can leave them in the office, with the staff or give them to me."

"Gil," Sam called out, startling Lila. "I want to make a donation." He looked down at her. "C'mon, honey. Come with me, because I'm doing this for you," he whispered.

Surprised, she let him take her hand and she

followed as they went up steps and crossed the small stage to Gil.

Sam pulled a piece of paper out of his pocket. "I want to make a donation for the child-care center."

"Sam Gordon is making the first donation for the center," Gil announced, waving Sam's check as the audience cheered and applauded. Raising his hand for quiet, Gil glanced down to read Sam's check. Wide-eyed, he looked at Sam. "You're sure?" he asked in a hushed tone.

"Very," Sam replied, smiling at Lila, and her curiosity grew while she braced for another of Sam's surprises.

Gil looked at the crowd and waved the check. "Folks, we have a generous donor who heartily supports the Texas Cattleman's Club's new child-care center. Sam Gordon donates one million dollars for the child-care center," Gil yelled, and the crowd broke into thunderous applause and cheers.

Stunned, Lila stared at him. "Sam…" she said.

"That's for you, Lila," he said quietly, while the noise of the crowd nearly drowned out what he said to her. She stared at him as people jostled her. They swarmed around him to shake his hand and

Lila got separated from him. She stepped back out of the way as people continued thanking him for his generous donation.

Smiling and laughing, he shook their hands. Some people hung back in silence on the fringe of the crowd, some bunching in small groups, and she recognized them and realized it was the men who had opposed the center so strongly, although she didn't see her dad in any of the groups and then he was there beside her with her mother at his side.

"That was a confounded-big donation Sam made tonight," Beau said. "Mom said she thinks Sam did that to please you." Beau had to raise his voice because of all the people nearby clustered around Sam who were still talking to him.

"Lila, what's going on with you two?" her father shouted over the noise. "Sam sends truckloads of flowers and makes this whopping donation to a cause he doesn't even like—"

"Isn't it great?" she asked, laughing and looking at her mother, who hugged her. "Dad, you're going to be a grandfather. We can talk about it tomorrow when I'm home."

"I'm what?" Beau said, blinking and staring openmouthed in one of the rare moments in her life when her father was speechless. He glanced at Barbara, who smiled and nodded. She leaned forward to hug Lila again and whisper in her ear.

"You picked a crazy time to tell him. Right now he can't say much of anything to you and it'll give him time to adjust to the idea a little. I don't mind fielding questions."

"Thanks, Mom."

"Be good to Sam. You have one million reasons to, for the sake of the child-care center and the children who will be in it. And for your own good."

"I'm flabbergasted. In a lifetime, I would never have guessed Sam Gordon would do any such thing."

"Nor would I, but I told you, Sam's a good man. Lila, for a million, he has to be crazy in love," she said in Lila's ear because the noise around them was still chaotic.

Lila stared at her mother and then turned to hug her dad, who squinted at her. "Damnation. I'm going to be a grandfather?" he shouted.

"That's right," she said loudly, smiling broadly. "You may be glad for this center someday. Now, I need to go speak to Sam."

"Lila," Beau snapped, beginning to pull himself together. His face flushed and he narrowed his eyes. "Lila—" he began again, but before he could say another word, she laughed, waved at him and moved through the crowd. The band began to play again and she glanced up to see Sam looking her way. People were still shaking his hand and talking to him.

Finally, he was there in front of her. Before she could hug him or thank him, he grabbed her arm. "Let's go," he said, and moved ahead to lead the way to the nearest door.

In minutes they were in the car, driving toward Pine Valley. She unfastened her seat belt to hug Sam's neck.

"Hey, Lila," he said, laughing and pulling over to the curb.

"Thank you, Sam Gordon. I'm speechless and awed and sorry I ever doubted you."

"Buckle up again and we'll talk when we're in a better place."

She sat back and fastened her seat belt. "Sam, that is the most wonderful thing. I'm thrilled and I know everyone who wants the center is, also. That will pay off the debt on the center and do the things we still need to have done."

"I did that for you, Lila. The money should take care of everything, and what's left can go for more supplies for the kids. Whatever they need."

"I can't believe you did that."

"We'll talk about my reasons when we get to my place."

"I'll warn you now—in that crowd I finally told my dad that I'm pregnant."

"You what?" Sam snapped, frowning and glancing at her. "Maybe I better pull over again."

"No, you keep driving. I want to get to your house. As for Dad, I didn't tell him who the father is. Not yet."

"He can figure that one out. He's probably gone home to get his shotgun."

She smiled, feeling better, but she was beginning to face reality again and in spite of his donation, she would still tell Sam goodbye tonight. "Actually, for one of the rare moments in my life, my dad was speechless. I told him in that crowd and he just stared at me with his mouth hanging open. Mom thought it was funny. She said she would answer his questions."

"Your mom is a good sport."

"Yes, she is, to put up with my dad all these years."

"I can't believe you did that. He'll know now why I've sent you so many flowers."

"Oh, yes, he will, but he can't really do anything about it."

"Damn, Lila, what a time to tell him. He's probably looking for me now."

"I thought it the perfect time to tell him. He was very impressed by your donation, and Mom told him you did that for me, so he was trying to absorb that bit of information."

Sam shook his head as he drove. The drive to his house seemed interminable, but eventually they arrived and soon she walked into an empty hallway while Sam switched on lights.

"Finally," she said, wrapping her arms around his neck and standing on tiptoe. "You did that for me," she said. "Sam, thank you." She looked into his blue eyes and saw desire as he looked at her mouth.

"Lila, I've wanted you more than you can possibly imagine," he whispered, and leaned down to kiss her.

The moment his lips touched hers, all thought fled. She forgot the donation, her resolutions about getting over her feelings for Sam and everything else that evening. Sam wrapped an arm tightly around her waist and pulled her close against him, leaning over so she had to cling to him.

Her hips thrust against him. She hugged him tightly, kissing him with all the pent-up longing that seemed to burst into flames within her. Excitement made her tremble as she held him and kissed him.

Desire enveloped her, sweeping away thought, logic—everything except a need to hold and love him. She began to twist free the buttons on his shirt, her fingers fumbling the task in her haste. She felt his hands on her clothes and then cool air on her bare shoulders.

As they shed clothes, he walked her backward along the hall. Finally, he picked her up and carried her to a downstairs bedroom, setting her on her feet and switching on a small lamp that shed a pale glow on them. She kicked off her shoes as he did the same and then she reached for him, walking into his arms. He held her away a moment to look at her before he began to shower kisses over her, his hands caressing her.

She moaned softly with pleasure, trailing her fingers over his hard muscles, tangling them in his chest hair. "Sam, I want you."

He framed her face with his hands and she opened her eyes to look at him, starting to lean forward to kiss him again, but he stopped her.

"Lila, I want to say this when you know it's not in a moment of passion where I'm not thinking about what I'm telling you," he whispered. "I'm focused, coherent and absolutely certain. Darlin', I love you. I need you in my life."

His words were another stunning surprise. Searching his face, she gazed into his wide eyes, which held desire and tenderness, a look that melted her heart. "Oh, Sam," she whispered.

"I love you, darlin'," he repeated.

"Oh, my love," she whispered. "What will we

do?" she asked, wanting his love yet knowing it would complicate their lives and a future together was impossible. "I can't, Sam—"

He silenced her, kissing her passionately while his hands roamed over her, caressing her, stirring desire. Clinging to him, she kissed him, pouring out all the love she felt for him.

"We'll love again, long and slow, but this time, Lila, I can't wait," he whispered, and picked her up. Looking into his eyes, she wrapped her long legs around him while he lowered her to his thick rod, entering her slowly.

Gasping with pleasure and need, Lila held him tightly, closing her eyes and drowning in sensation. He eased slowly into her and then his thrusts were faster. Clinging to his broad shoulders, wrapped around him and still not close enough, she moved with him as need built swiftly.

"I love you, Sam," she whispered without thinking about it, immersed totally in awareness of his body with hers, driven to seek satisfaction.

She moved faster, finally crying out with a release that carried her into blinding rapture.

"Ahh, Sam. I love you," she whispered again,

scattering light kisses on his face. She held him tightly until finally he set her on her feet and then kissed her gently as he held her in his arms.

Sam carried her to a bathroom and they showered together between long kisses. After they had dried, he disappeared and came back with two robes, handing a white one to her while he pulled on a navy.

He picked her up to walk to a sofa in a family area and sat with her on his lap. She gazed into his incredible blue eyes and kissed him softly. "I love you, Sam."

"Lila, that's the very best news of all. I love you, too, darlin'. I made that donation for you, Lila. I voted against the children's center and I didn't want it, but I wouldn't do anything to stop it. If you want it, darlin', then I suppose I want it."

"That's the sweetest thing I ever heard. You don't have to want something because I do and the donation was the most wonderful gift," she said, laughing and hugging him. "I'm still shocked."

"Lila, will you marry me?" he asked.

Her smile faded as she looked into his eyes while having a dull ache in her heart. "Some things haven't changed. I don't want to give up my career and come back to Royal. I love you with all my heart, but I can't do that. At least not at this point in my life. I may change my mind later."

He kissed her lightly and then looked into her eyes. "You don't have to come back to Royal. We'll work something out. I'd rather have part of you than none of you."

"You'll live in Royal and I'll live in California? Do you really think that will work?"

"I'm working on it, Lila," he said, suddenly becoming solemn. "I've thought about Roddy's talk. He wants to hire me to build his house. He would have contacts. He said he had a film project he would like to hire me for. That's a big start. I can open a branch in L.A."

She felt as if she couldn't breathe and her head spun. "You would do that for me?" she asked, staring at him. "You do love me," she whispered.

"Yes, I do. And yes, I would do that for you. I want to be with you. I have money invested and saved up and we inherited Dad's money—"

Flinging her arms around his neck, she let out a shriek that stopped his words. Smiling, he brushed her hair away from her face. "Lila, you're part of my life. I just want to be with you. Darlin', you captured my heart completely."

Tears of joy filled her eyes. "Sam, that is the most wonderful thing you could say or do." She showered kisses on his face, running her hands across his shoulders. "What about your brother?"

"I don't think we'll take him with us," Sam replied with a twinkle in his eyes.

"You know what I mean. What about leaving Josh?"

"Josh can run the business here. We each go our own ways and we can fly back and forth whenever we want because we each have our own plane. There's no problem there for me. If one develops, I'll tell you. But, darlin', I want to be where you want to be."

She kissed him and then leaned back. "I love you, love you, love you," she said between kisses. "I'm so happy. Yes, I'll marry you."

"You will?" he asked, grinning suddenly. "Wahoo!" he threw back his head and yelled, making her laugh. "Darlin', I'm the happiest man on earth at this moment. Hooray!" he shouted. He stood up to take a step away and stopped abruptly. He placed one hand on her waist and reached into the pocket of his robe. "Hold out your hand. I have something for you."

"Sam, is my life going to be just one big surprise after another? What are you doing now?"

"Hold out your hand, darlin'," he said. When she did, he placed a tiny package in her hand. It was blue tissue paper tied with a pink silk ribbon.

"What on earth, Sam?" She was curious because if it had been jewelry, she would have expected a box, but it was too tiny for anything else. She untied the bow and pushed open the tissue paper to find a ring with dazzling diamonds surrounding an emerald-cut stone. He picked it up to hold it out to her.

"This is the tiniest token of what I feel for you. It represents my love and my commitment to you and to our family together. It's forever, Lila. I love you with all my being."

"Sam, that is the sweetest thing," she said, getting a knot in her throat and feeling tears of joy forming. "I love you so much. I tried to avoid you and I just never could. From that first night, you captured my heart."

He drew her to him to kiss her. She closed her fist over the ring and put her arm around his neck to return his kiss, wanting him again and loving him more than she would have thought possible.

After a long kiss, she looked up. "Now I have something for you—some news that will give you something else to shout about," she said, smiling at him.

"What's that?" he asked. "I don't think anything could possibly be as important as the fact that we're in love, we're getting married and we're having a baby."

"Oh, yes, there is something, Sam. You talked me into seeing a doctor in Royal, but you never asked me about my appointment."

Sam's smile faded away. "I never saw you that week. You're all right, aren't you?" he asked.

"I'm quite all right. You were partially correct when you said that we're in love and we're getting married. But we're not having a baby, exactly."

Sam frowned. "Lila," he said in a threatening voice. "How can you not have a baby exactly?"

Laughing, she gazed up at him. "Sam, we're having two babies—twin girls."

He blinked and stared at her a moment and then he stepped back and jumped in the air, throwing up his arms while he let out a yell loud enough to make her put her hands over her ears while she laughed. "Wahoo!" he yelled again. "If you weren't pregnant, I'd pick you up and spin you around with me."

"Don't you dare," she said, laughing at him as she spoke.

"Twin girls. Lila, that's the most fantastic news. I have to call Josh right now and tell him."

"Come here, Sam, and don't be ridiculous. He's still at the party at the club."

"I don't care where he is. You've told your dad that you're pregnant, so I think I need to call and ask him for your hand in marriage."

"Now, there's my old-fashioned lover popping out finally," she said.

"Oh, yes. You also have an old-fashioned dad—I believe you've informed me of that a few dozen times. I'm definitely calling him to ask for your hand in marriage. I should have before I proposed, but I'm not so traditional about everything. I'd go see him first, but I think I'd better place a call. I'll just have him paged at the party."

"Paged? Sam, this will be all over Royal by the time you get off the phone."

He grinned, hugging her. "Yes, it will, darlin'. I can't wait for everyone to know. Twins. Ahh, Lila, I love you so. It's going to be wonderful, darlin'."

"I think so, too," she said, smiling at him. He kissed her again and then took her hand.

"Let's go to the kitchen and I'll get that hot chocolate. Then I'll make my calls. I can put the phone on speaker if you'd like to hear what's said."

Smiling, she shook her head. "Thanks, I'll pass on that one. This is a man-to-man thing in both cases. I may be glad I'll fly out of here Monday."

As she sat in Sam's kitchen and sipped hot chocolate, she listened to him call her dad on his cell phone and ask for permission to marry her. Thinking Sam's call was ridiculous but sweet, she smiled at him. Finally, Sam ended his call.

"He is overjoyed and I'm guessing enormously relieved to find that we are getting married. Now

I'm going to page Josh and tell him. This will shake up his world a bit."

"Not too much. They're your twins, not his."

She listened as Sam had his brother paged and she covered her face. If she didn't go to church tomorrow, she wouldn't see anyone except her family before she flew to California and when she came back again, she and Sam would be old news.

"Josh, Sam. Yeah, I'm okay," he said. "Keep your shirt on. You can go back to the party in a few minutes. I have news." There was a pause before he continued. "It can't wait until tomorrow. I asked Lila to marry me and she said yes."

She guessed Josh said congratulations and was probably still scratching his head over why Sam couldn't wait until tomorrow to tell him.

"I want you to be best man when we marry." She smiled again at Sam, because he was probably already planning their wedding.

"Yeah, there's something else. You're going to be an uncle."

She heard another loud yell, surprising her because Josh had always seemed more serious and controlled than Sam. Words poured out, but she couldn't understand what Josh was saying. "That's right, twin girls. Yeah, we'll celebrate."

Lila listened to one side of the conversation a few more minutes and then Sam finished his call. "He's excited. So is your dad."

"I'm surprised at two bachelors being so thrilled over becoming a dad and an uncle. Especially two bachelors who fought the child-care center."

"That was a whole different thing, and maybe Josh and I are ready for some family in our lives. I know I am," he said, leaning close to kiss her lightly. "Next time, sugar, I want to be the first to know—after you, of course. I forgot I wasn't supposed to call you *sugar,* but you know it's because I love you."

"You can call me whatever you want," she said, smiling at him and then looking at her ring. "This is a gorgeous ring. I love it."

"And I love you. I can't tell you enough." He moved his chair and reached out to pick her up and place her on his lap. "This is so good, Lila. You've made me happy beyond my wildest dreams. I'm the happiest man on earth. Two little girls. Our twin daughters. We'll be doubly blessed."

"I think so. I'm overjoyed and you're not so old-fashioned after all, I guess. Since it's twins, I might even think about cutting back a little on my work. Working at home or something while they're babies. The doctor told me to think about maternity leave, too, before I have them."

"Good. Lila, love, not in my wildest dreams did I expect this. It's the most awesome thing to happen to me."

He wrapped her in his arms and pulled her close to kiss her. She held him tightly, knowing he was the love of her life, now and always. With Sam, her future would be filled with joy and love and a precious family.

* * * * *